Adva

'Ahalya, Draup[adi...] of the *Pancha Kanyas* is fascinating. Ahalya's story has been told and retold several times, sometimes with varying accounts across texts. What was her relationship with Gautam and Indra? What was her crime? How was she redeemed? Why is she among the Pancha Kanyas? There have been modern retellings and interpretations too. Koral Dasgupta's wonderful retelling adds to this corpus, with a lyrical and poetic quality. The image that will remain with you is of the Mist. That is the reason *Ahalya*, and this rendition, is so enthralling' – **Bibek Debroy**

'"Go woman, find your world yourself. The joy you seek deserves to be discovered." Armed with this advice, Ahalya sets off on her life's journey. The magical and thought-provoking adventure that follows will intrigue and mesmerize readers' – **Chitra Banerjee Divakaruni**

'Koral Dasgupta's evocation of Ahalya, the first of the Pancha Kanyas, the five virtuous women from Indian myth, is an enigmatic tale about purity, chastity, seduction, and redemption, told from the perspective of the eternal feminine' – **Namita Gokhale**

'Amazing premise and approach. This is one unique take on an age-old tale. Brilliant and intriguing'
– **Anand Neelakantan**

AHALYA

KORAL DASGUPTA is an author, painter, entrepreneur and professor. She is a compulsive storyteller and has authored four books which include three works of fiction and a non-fiction on Bollywood. Her fourth book has been optioned for screen adaptation. She is the founder of www.tellmeyourstory.biz, a story ecosystem led by crowd-sourced narratives. She consults with educational and corporate organizations on content and communication projects. Koral is recognized in the list of Innovator25 Asia Pacific 2019 prepared by The Holmes Report. Her website is http://koraldasgupta.com.

Forthcoming in the Sati Series

Kunti
Draupadi
Mandodari
Tara

AHALYA

KORAL DASGUPTA

THE SATI SERIES

PAN

First published 2020 by Pan
an imprint of Pan Macmillan Publishing India Private Limited
707, Kailash Building,
26, K. G. Marg, New Delhi – 110 001
www.panmacmillan.co.in

The Smithson, 6 Briset Street, London EC1M 5NR
Associated companies throughout the world
www.panmacmillan.com

ISBN 978-93-89109-66-5

Copyright © Koral Dasgupta 2020

This is a work of fiction. Names, characters, businesses, organizations, places, events, and incidents either are the product of the author's imagination or are used fictiously. Any resemblance to actual persons, living or dead, events, or locales is entirely coincidental.

All rights reserved. No part of this publication may be reproduced, stored in or introduced into a retrieval system, or transmitted, in any form, or by any means (electronic, mechanical, photocopying, recording or otherwise) without the prior written permission of the publisher. Any person who does any unauthorized act in relation to this publication may be liable to criminal prosecution and civil claims for damages.

3 5 7 9 8 6 4 2

This book is sold subject to the condition that it shall not, by way of trade or otherwise, be lent, re-sold, hired out, or otherwise circulated without the publisher's prior consent in any form of binding or cover other than that in which it is published and without a similar condition including this condition being imposed on the subsequent purchaser.

Typeset in Guardi LT Std by R. Ajith Kumar, New Delhi
Printed in India by Gopsons Papers Pvt. Ltd., Noida

For my son, Neev Tanish

CONTENTS

Ahalya 1

A Note to the Readers 199
Acknowledgements 202

PROLOGUE

In the middle of a dark stormy night, lightning struck and cracked the sky into millions of fragments. Unruly winds invaded the Earth, crushing everything that came in their way; in the absence of anything else to clash on, they collided against each other, laughing wildly at their own wreckage. A huge neem tree outside our window fell to the damp ground with a loud thrash, a sound as terrible as a demonic attack on mankind. Scared, I had clung on to my mother, my strongest grip alarmingly weak. She too was in panic but kept that confused heart under wraps of tenderness. She held me with warmth, assuring that we were safe and not dying that night. The fall of the tree was symbolic, prophesying the most farcical times to follow. Stripped of its modesty, our humble clay house now stood bare, shamelessly available to the slithering eyes of the passers-by, the after-effects of the calamity ridiculing its nude display.

Just like I stand now, barren and powerless. Mother being miles apart, lost somewhere in the manipulations of history, unheeding to my most anxious prayers.

❋

I am one of those unfortunate ones who has witnessed her own birthing process, measure by measure. As indistinct as a particle of faint light, the soul floating restlessly amidst the feathery clouds asked, *Why?* Brahma, the Father, was engrossed in his magical world, still absorbed in the designs of that perfect body which was soon meant to shelter me. In a large metallic tub he put white stone, sandalwood, mahogany, rose petals and lotus leaves. With a huge black rock chiselled like a cylinder supported on his shoulders, he ran around the tub to crush the ingredients into a fine powder, awakening the world below with his footsteps and disrupting the heavenly slumber with resounding deformation.

'Who am I, Father?' I asked again.

'The face of my ambitions.' He declared, beaming with the arrogance of patriarchy, striving to achieve one of his many aspirations through the perfection of the progeny. 'You would be the most beautiful one; enigmatic and graceful. The four worlds – *Svarga*, *Martya*, *Akash*, and *Pataal*[1] – would stand apart watching you, walking in glory as Brahma's most magnificent creation.'

He picked up a sample of the powder grinded into the metallic tub to inspect closely if any granule had been left unattended. He crushed them again, and then again, to form a perfectly dry mixture. The dark of mahogany blended with the white of sandalwood and stone. Rose

---

[1] Svarga: Heaven; Martya: Earth; Akash: Space; and Pataal: Underworld.

petals added a pink hue. Lotus leaves nourished it with their oil. The final content looked fair and shiny now. Brahma let out a sharp joyful glee and stretched his aching arms. The soul allowed him to relish the euphoria sweeping through all corners of his heart. Then softly and hesitantly it tried to present the inherent dilemma.

'How fair is it, Father, that I stand here like a spirit, watching my body getting meticulously sculpted?'

'You wouldn't have if there were a mother to host you in her womb.' Brahma uttered with indifference. 'Your intelligence would then have merged with that of the mother, your responses would have been minutely attended to with all diligence, your comfort being her absolute priority. In the womb the soul remains dormant, oblivious of the growth that will eventually gravitate towards light.'

He picked up a spade and ventured out without waiting for a probable response. The soul followed him.

'What is a mother?' I probed.

'A mother is another name for unyielding, aggressive power. She is the embodiment of indulgence and restraint. She is the keeper, the protector. She restricts to keep all harm away. She beholds the baby with her softness, yet forms a tough cast around it to keep intruders at bay. She is the first teacher starting the learning process in confinement, by sharing the system of body and life even before the baby is born. She is the form of knowledge that results from reflex.'

With great force Brahma hit the ground with his spade. The rigid surface ruptured and smooth, mushy soil burst from beneath. With quick strokes he picked the soil with the spade and shoved it aside to be carried back to his cryptic cave where the metal tub was waiting with an insatiable appetite.

'And father?' The word appeared spontaneously after the analysis he gave of mother. I wasn't sure what relationship did bind the two so deep that one wasn't complete without the other. Brahma seemed to be as affected as I by this bizarre inevitable connection.

'Father's knowledge results from experience. The father is the risk-taker. He is the more tranquil form of power. He seeks perfection in his child while the mother finds perfection in her child. If on some occasion his child is unhappy, the father can deal with it. He stands by to support it through its pain. The mother is always eager to find a way out and source happiness for her child from depths beyond her reach. She is never ready to accept that her solutions may not work. And …'

'Why don't I have a mother?' I interrupted, unwilling to spend time on futile arguments in favour of fathers. My incessant queries had crossed the line of desperation. Brahma looked up with a cold calm, his eyes still as glass.

'Because you are not born out of a man's carnal desires. You are the brilliance of my imagination, not the inheritance of karma. You are the grandeur of an artist who instils life on the white of a blank canvas. You will be the unique commitment of an enterprising painter and would eventually be celebrated by admirers. You can't have parents because you are the unidimensional face of the father's pleasure, not the mother's pain. You will attract a million suitors obsessing over the beauty I craft with care, but the same beauty will be too blinding for a lover to trace the path to your soul.'

It sounded depressing! Slowly I moved away, leaving Brahma alone with his mystical prophecies. Like the spunky serpent spiralling towards its charmer I floated around in haste, determined to find myself a mother. But no one wanted to cross their paths with Brahma.

'He's a sage,' said the River, her expanse delightfully dancing through the pebbles. 'The ripples on my body and the curves of my banks are of no use to him. When he walks in to quench his thirst the edges parch with his radiance. The soft soil along the banks – my love child with the shadowy mountain – looks back naked and dehydrated, demanding to know why it's being punished. I can't mother Brahma's daughter. He is too distant, too unbending towards the fantasies of the feminine. It's more dignified to lash on a rock and disperse into broken droplets than engaging with Brahma.'

Swirling away from her I approached the Rain. 'Your Mother? Brahma's wife?' She winced in sarcasm as the plains turned white with ghastly downpour. Lightning cracked across the sky, intimidating winds abused the trees, a thousand ghosts laughed from behind the black clouds. 'He is the kind of man who is obsessed with the influence of his own capacities. He can coexist without conflict as long as his knowledge isn't questioned and his judgement isn't debated. Brahma is driven by neither mind nor heart; it's only his brain that amuses itself with his creations of timeless wonders! I have tried to soak him in pleasure as he walked through these terrains. I have demanded him to stop with all my might. I have caused him distress with luscious distractions and ferocious interference. And yet he remains undeterred like the opaque of a rock! Your father is an insult to womanhood. He can't be pleased, nor can he be pleasured.'

These women wanted lovers. Not necessarily

a husband. They desired that their virtues be explored, their beauty appreciated, their seduction gratified. Motherhood blossoms out of love for the lover. A child born from loveless union is such a disaster! Thrown between parents who don't celebrate their togetherness, the child suffers a lack of emotional identity and a sense of belonging. I, a result of neither passion nor compulsion, was perhaps a bigger castaway. My father called me his work of art. Hasn't the world always attended with vengence to every form of creativity that is beyond one's comprehension?

1

Wandering all alone once again, demoralized and defeated, I rested on the topmost branch of Kalpavriksha. The Tree of Life, that fulfilled the wishes of all, looked up with curious bewilderment. The soft green leaves quivered with vigour. Pretty little orange flowers appeared as buds and soon bloomed, dew dribbling down the tips of the petals and the centres pregnant with pollen. Petite blue birds appeared from nowhere and flocked from flower to flower in search for nectar, playfully nudging and outwitting each other. So beautiful was this happiness beneath. And such depressing was the nothingness above. Droplets smeared around. Mortals had a name for them – 'tears' – I learnt much later.

The birds and flowers and leaves looked distant now. Their chirrups still audible but vision blurred. I straightened myself. A smooth cloudy steam had enveloped me. The Mist.

'You aren't permitted to do this!' she whispered in my ear.

Confused, I tried to comprehend what command I had violated! Before I asked, the Mist spoke again.

'You can't cry. If Brahma comes to know he will disown you even before he completes your birthing process.'

'What would that mean?' I asked, unsure of what I wanted to know.

The Mist seemed ruthless with her knowledge, unwilling to restrict with herself what was not to be told. 'If Brahma stops working on the body he is creating to cover you with, it would mean a terrible curse. You will have to keep floating timelessly like an undesired homeless soul, which can neither live nor die. You will have the power to interpret everything, yet you would be powerless to bring about any change. You will exist, but you will not be seen. You will be honoured only with a ghostly presence and earthlings will be scared of you, wondering about your evil dimensions. But the truth hidden from all is that you can't even harm them! You will belong nowhere. Heaven is for the Gods, Earth is for the living creatures, Hell is where they go after death for the sins they had committed in life. A cursed soul has no space to call its own.'

I recoiled in denial. *No! What blunder have I committed to invite such a fateful non-existence? Why would Father abandon me like a defective caricature? What act of mine could irk him to this extent?*

The Mist read my despondency before I had made myself heard. 'The soul must not cry,' she said. 'The soul should not emote. The soul can't have a heart. The soul is supposed to be free – unattached, companionless, yet complete.' The moist shelter of the Mist cuddled me like a baby. Perhaps this is how a mother caresses the unborn child from the outer cast of her inflated belly and the child knows it's being loved. I too felt loved, embraced by the foggy cover.

'Let's go from here,' she advised.

'Why?' I asked, surprised.

'There's a storm approaching. The eastern sky is black. Hungry forces are on their way.'

I tried to listen. Life seemed peaceful. Through the translucent layers of the Mist I could see the birds and the flowers. Where were the destructive winds? What was this dubious code of the cosmos?

'Let's go,' the Mist repeated, this time with authority. I floated again reluctantly towards the northwest; the Mist floated with me, still surrounding me like a balloon. After moments of stoic silence when I could contain myself no more, the foggy presence came closer inviting me for an affectionate hug.

'The visuals you experienced were illusions. There were no flowers with pollen, no birds gayfully singing songs of spring. The sound of violent winds that you didn't hear was the only truth.'

Shocked beyond measure, questions piled up one over another. The Mist explained with empathy.

'Kalpavriksha or Kalpataru emerged from the primal waters during Samudra Manthan.[2] Indra, the King of Gods, brought it to Heaven and planted it there. Indra, the majestic and handsome one, is also the God of Illusions. The moment you came in contact with Kalpavriksha, the divine manifested. You perceived beauty, you shed tears, much before your creator had instilled these powers in you. So absorbed you were in that illusion that the threats from the east couldn't reach you. You were treading the path of severe destructions.'

I was too naive to understand what she spoke. I asked something else, something that had eroded my confidence to ashes. 'Can Father really leave me undone? Can he be so cruel?'

---

[2] The great churning of the ocean is an episode in Hindu mythology, which explains the ocean to be the origin of many jewels, divine animals, flowers, plants, weapons and tools along with *amrita*, the drink of immortality.

The Mist sighed a heavy fog of breath. 'Yes, he can. No man likes his convictions to be confronted. Brahma desires unconditional devotion from his offspring,' she smiled. 'With you though he is even more cautious.'

'Why?' Each passing moment some new realization was dawning upon me. I was learning something not only about myself but also about my creator.

'You are your father's dream, not the dictum of fate. So even Brahma can't foresee your future. He would have to come to terms with it along with you, accepting the rules of life as it unfolds its mystery. He can only create your body, not your birth chart. You will have to write your own future. Such lack of control makes him nervous.' It didn't make much sense to me. An insecure confusion throbbed restlessly.

'Has he ever left a soul unattended before?' I never wanted to bring this up; it came on its own. And once a question appears it will find its answer anyway. Here, the Mist offered to clarify with tremendous honesty every doubt that raised its head and left it to me to host the battle between acceptance and denial.

'Yes, he does that often, especially with humans.' The Mist crushed all hope that expected to hear about a kind-hearted Father. 'When a human being is born on Earth, Brahma starts planning the next birth. After death they reach Hell to absolve themselves of their sins, and thereafter reach Brahma with absolute innocence when refurbished into their new bodies. Their life chart is reconstructed by Brahma, their purpose on Earth refabricated.'

The Mist paused to look at me closely as I stared in awe. She spoke again. 'Earthlings are strange creatures. They try to correct the decisions of God seeking help of astrology. They aim to manipulate birth, life and death, stealing through the preconstructed diagrams. Sometimes, unwilling to bear their share of the earthly burden, they try to end their lives before Brahma had willed. Enraged, he curses them and leaves them in limbo. The souls thus float around desperately, unclaimed and futureless, till

Brahma calms down and includes them back in his creative queue.'

Having reached the cave where Father was engrossed in his magical art, the Mist stood facing me.

Would you come again? I didn't ask, but I received my answer nevertheless.

'Stay prepared for a long journey ahead. And remember, I am your biggest secret. I am your most potent strength. Today. And always.'

I didn't offer the Mist to mother me, yet she became one. She protected, cared for and loved me. She nurtured and nourished me. In the days that followed she covered for my adventures and took responsibilities upon herself, setting me free to play out in the wild. The only truth she kept from me was that she was another incarnation of the same illusion sent across as messenger by the sensuous, charismatic Indra!

This I learnt much, much later.

I left the Mist outside and entered the magic cave of the Creator. Walls made of thin ice, the outside world was visible from inside the cave.

But not a drop of water trickled down its stern surface, not even in broad daylight when merciless sun rays blazed through each day only to return in defeat each evening. No outsider was permitted until Father himself extended the invite. Chunks of snow would form a spear at the entrance at the minutest effort to violate this custom.

I looked behind to check on the Mist. She was gone. A droning sound welcomed me from the other end. Father was crafting me, slowly, scattering flakes of sandalwood all around. Steady hands were carving the designs with confidence. Stealthily, I walked up to him and stared at the body. The face seemed as notorious as the Rain, the body voluptuous like the River, and the dense and overpowering hair like the Mist! Strong eyebrows, broad forehead and a small chin on an oval face, with eyes closed into a lifeless sleep carried a distinct smirk which Brahma would not have added deliberately. But such, I have learnt from Father, is the indomitable spirit of creation. You can create only a part of your vision; the rest creates itself!

Brahma stood erect and poured honey from a barrel. The sticky liquid dropped slowly on the forehead, then made its way downwards, glistening the crust and adding a brownish tinge with its golden viscosity. He dragged a huge basket from the other end of the cave. In it freshly plucked marigolds and jasmines sparkled like stars, their natural delight energizing the gloomy silence inside the cave. With enormous patience Brahma covered the honey-washed body with these flowers, the yellow and white petals sticking to the skin like a rich amorphous cover.

Brahma fell on the ground, exhausted.

'The flowery cover looks weird,' I couldn't help reacting.

'Why do you say that?' Brahma raised his head.

'I am not sure. But the sight feels awkward, I don't know why!' I floated around mischievously, inspecting Brahma's work like a critic.

Brahma's stern eyes locked themselves over me, trying to discover the source of my discomfort. Unable to trace a clue from my restless movements around the body, he sighed.

'Human bodies are covered with flowers after death, before they are cremated. That's why the sight isn't bringing to you the best of vibes. A lot is same about the stages before birth and after death. But I wonder how this knowledge has come over to trouble you well before your entry into the process of life! Maybe the consciousness of death precedes the awareness of birth.'

The curves of the body were apparent under the heavy floral cover.

'Will I be a woman, Father?' I asked, attempting to divert Brahma from the deep philosophical mess I had thrown him into. He stumped me back.

'What do you know about being a woman?' This time his voice was affectionate. A faint smile lurked around the corners of his lips. Or so I felt. But the question he posed was far more confusing than the sudden unexpected fondness. What did I know about being a woman? Nothing, actually!

I wasn't familiar with any specific trait, habit or behaviour which remains confined within this tribe called 'woman'. The word invoked warmth and tenderness. Some impressions were cast so strong that I could feel its dimensions clearly but explaining in words was cumbersome. I fumbled.

'You are a woman already,' I heard the Creator speak. 'A seeker of truth. A follower of the divine. And a victim of her own intimidating strength. After your birthing is complete you will also soon learn the skills of a manipulator who attempts to encrust the reality in a shield of affection and beauty.' Brahma smiled again.

'That means I shall be pretty and nice?' My novice curiosity had perhaps started unsettling the four-headed God. He grew serious.

'Yes. More than that. Ahalya, you will be named', he said without caring to look up. 'Ahalya, meaning, the unploughed, the unaffected, the untouched. The one who is pure. The one who doesn't carry any baggage from her earlier births. Who isn't followed by karma, who can't be tamed by destiny. The one whose sanctity can be altered by none.'

Once again I floated around free as Brahma returned to his mystic tools, keeping himself engrossed with his artistic impressions. The body had by then absorbed the honey and juices from the flower petals. It looked moisturised; the rough wooden surface felt visibly softer and glistened with nourishment.

Late at night Brahma's rumbles meddled with the hymn of crickets introducing loneliness to melancholy. Wisdom floated around like decayed leaves with every breath of Father. Usually, I play with them. I blow them apart. I tease. I chase. But today was different. I hadn't smelt those little orange flowers, but I knew the fragrance. Somewhat rugged and erotic, it felt adventurous. Reckless and raunchy. They bloomed to their fullest and inched closer to me as if they had been held together in a bouquet. As if they were the greetings of Nature. As if the soft feathery petals would have pleasured my skin if I could touch them. And the fact that I couldn't left them insatiated as much as it made me feel deprived. When the Mist pulled me away they must have stared from behind, longing for my return. My sudden retreat must have felt disgraceful towards the beauty that willingly came to serve but wasn't allowed to fulfil its task. The blue birds may have followed me to warn that I was leaving behind an incomplete saga, that this moment would be lost forever in the conspiracy of time. The sigh of the orange flowers would curse my giving in future as my gifts will also be insulted with indifference. The chirpy little beings were perhaps stopped abruptly at the entrance of Brahma's cave as icy spears threatened them of dire consequences.

From inside the cave I found the Moon diving into the enormous space. A string of stars clumsily attached to his hands settled themselves in their pre-scheduled positions as soon as the crescent arched to find its balance. The insides of the dark cave lit up. The Moon was the only fearless being who dared to peep inside Brahma's cave with eerie notoriety, albeit from a distance. As much the snow thickened to mar its transparency, the bright silvery rays permeated, creating obnoxious shadows on the floor. He laughed as the patterns made a mockery of all attempts to privacy. What a strange war of might!

2

Days and nights passed. I wandered alone and at times enveloped by the Mist. We floated together over valleys and mountains, watching life prosper and progress at its own pace. The Mist narrated stories of Indra like a lullaby on balmy afternoons and folklore on breezy evenings. Voice echoing like thunder, eyes red with fury, muscular body held erect, gallantly riding on his celestial horse Uchchaishravas – vivid descriptions played clandestine images in my dreams. The warrior was set to kill the *asura* Vritra, who was obstructing human happiness by holding captive all sources of water. The war cry by the King of Gods had shaken the underworld, threatening to uproot it with all its vice and scatter the leftovers in the bottomless pit to fall perennially.

Long strands of hair flowing behind, strong arms determined to destroy the monstrous filth, mouth carved to announce heroic victory – I could almost visualize the King of Gods at war to return life to the thirsty Earth.

The Mist also narrated tales of his lovers, flickering obsessively with insomniac desires, waiting to be pleasured by his hypnotic manoeuvres. 'So powerful are his ploys of seduction that there isn't a woman who wouldn't fantasize her presence in Indra's chambers. He plays with a woman as a child does with water. He would pick her up tenderly with both his hands, cup her face in his palms and touch her with his lips. He would let her explore far beyond the lips just like water drips on your neck and chest when you drink with impatience. He would throw himself upon her, bathing through the sea of luxury, unwilling to release till every inch of his being is soaked in the rhythm of his mistress.'

Almost sailing in the reverie of a majestic king's sensuous practices, the word abruptly halted my fancies. 'Mistress?' I uttered in dismay.

'Indeed. Mistress they are,' confirmed the Mist. 'Making love with Indra inflicts such weariness on his women that they fall into a timeless sleep, recovering only after he has left them for good. Only Saachi, his wife, is blessed to match up to his passionate energies. No one else.'

'And Indra?' I asked softly, unwilling to let this conversation end too soon. But the Mist was smarter.

'He is the ever insatiable one.'

She said and disappeared, leaving me alone with my fantasies. Maybe she could see that I was on the edge of desperation to seek Indra and pose before him the most impossible challenge of the cosmos. Would the lustful King of Devas, desirous of and desired by the universe, like to explore the faceless? Can he touch in the absence of skin? Can he pleasure the one without a body? Would the greatest lover known for his rugged energies make love with this soul?

That evening when I returned to Brahma's cave I found him standing there with a rare happiness shining through his body. He gestured towards a lifeless figure lying on the ground, her body smelling of sandalwood, her complexion close to ivory with a hint of rose. The honey and floral extracts had settled on her upper crust adding hue and shine. Though lifeless and rigid on the surface, the body seemed to possess the essence of rare vigour, as if it were made to spark a revolution!

'This is perfect, Father,' I gushed.

'Everyone is born perfect,' Brahma advised. 'They pick up the imperfections along the course of life.'

Father commanded me to lie atop her. I obeyed. His eyes glittered with ecstasy as I slowly merged with the tough exteriors of his sculpture. Almost immediately the wood softened and gave way to smooth, glistening skin. The nostrils breathed. The fingers quivered. The skin perched on to the new-found nerves and muscles as blood streamed through the veins. I felt the fascinating beats of my heart. A drop of tear trickled down my eye with the complex and painful consciousness of formally owning a body, though it lasted for no more than a few blinks. I sat up. Long, silky hair swept all over my back like waves.

A flood of light hit my eyes. I pulled my arm to block the rush and pushed backwards, covering my face with my hand. A strange fear of facing the unknown engulfed me. Fear, an emotion my soul was alien to but my body experienced within moments of its birth.

Battling with fear soon was the hopeless curiosity. I parted my slender fingers to peek. It was as dazzling but less blinding. Slowly I removed my hand and opened my eyes to the inevitable. This time the dash of energy didn't hurt. It touched with the affection of a grandfather, gauging my features. Perhaps to inspect their resemblance with the family I didn't have.

Piercing through the light a figure standing a few steps away slowly gained prominence. It was Brahma, my Father. When he didn't move I approached him with slow steps. I touched his feet. Satisfaction swept through his smile. He blessed me with a ray of satisfaction sweeping across his smile. 'You are free now, my child. Go fly, love, learn. Acquire wisdom and apply it. In pain and happiness, remember that nothing is absolute. Neither will last. Only you will, till the end of your time. Make the most of that.'

I had no interest in decoding the deep philosophy hidden in his words. I was restless to experience the universe all over again, this time with a more visible identity. With mirth that tinkled like a restless anklet, I rushed out to see myself on the still surface of the lake. The breeze played pranks, sending nasty ripples to muddle my image. I bent to view myself with the pry of a woman. Large eyes, full lips, long legs, thin waist – Brahma had created a magic portrait, too astounding to remain fitted into a bony frame. Gentle breeze passed through the unruly hair, combing them in order. Adding excitement to awe, I felt the tresses settling in compliance on my back, gently warning that the preparations for an eventful journey ahead had only started.

A warning that I heard but didn't pay any heed to.

I touched the water; large ripples spiralled out to celebrate my birth. As a human. As a woman. I turned to look towards the southeast where I had once rested myself on the divine Kalpavriksha. But before my vision reached there the Mist appeared rudely reproving the disobedience.

'You are just born, woman. Wait till you deserve what you desire,' she chided me.

Caught ruthlessly by Mother's protective ethics I turned away. She led me back to the cave.

The very next day I woke up with a realization that being hosted in a human form I no longer was entitled to the privileges that I had once enjoyed as a soul. I would have to leave Heaven!

'Where shall I go?' I turned towards the Mist.

'Human beings are held by rules and routines. They have to pursue what they want, what they desire. While they are bestowed with elevated powers to express anger, jealousy, joy, desperation, they are also deported from Heaven to live in exile, at a place called Earth, where sufferings manifest.'

With bated breath I waited for whatever was to follow. Early in the morning Father introduced me to a sage.

'Gautam,' he commanded. 'My most precious creation is now your responsibility. Take care of her, educate her, teach her the means and ends of life. Make sure she retains her sanctities as long as she is with you.'

Sanctity, I learnt from the Mist later, is a metaphysical way of remaining pure, godly. Pure at heart, pure in means and ends, pure by body, pure by faith. She called it 'Sati'. A pursuit to remain loyal and committed to one's truth and never deflect by greed or guile. To own up with conviction and turn away from deceit. To recognize the voice of the self without pretence and resist being touched by alien assassins inducing cynicism. To express with dignity, to comprehend in totality. To love without reservations. To give and not be affected by the pride of giving. To know, to value, to rise, to shine.

To find the joy of life in little nothings. To identify beauty in the mundane. To be Ahalya, who can be neither possessed nor forsaken.

I raised my eyes to look at Gautam.

Skin tanned, eyes like burnt charcoal, unruly hair, toned body wrapped in rugged shawls, Gautam nodded his head in acceptance of the command. His deathly cold felt scary. In human form he seemed more disciplined than the soul, perfectly in control of the task bestowed upon him but with no vested interest in reconciling with the jubilant zeal facing him. He lacked the domination of Father, nor did he have the compassion of the Mist. He stood in indifference and obedience, to be simply instructed and dismissed. Gautam's composure, in contrast with my new-born excitement, felt lifeless. He was thin and distant, his long, dishevelled hair tied into a loose knot. The breeze that had run through my strands to place them in order blew again, this time sending a shiver down my spine. The nervousness of uncertainty!

Unwilling to give in I tried to reason it out but

in vain. How would a destitute with no strength of arms or resources provide shelter to me? And why must he care? The pounding heart insecure of some offensive menace turned to Father to question why I couldn't stay with him. Brahma pronounced curtly. 'Since you have loved the beauty of being a human you have to face the consequences too. It's the balance that keeps the cosmos rolling. Nothing comes in isolation.' I shuddered inside, at the possibility of spending my days with a stranger. Why was my soul installed in an elegantly crafted body if I couldn't manifest in the magnificence of Heaven? Why should I be sent to the place where sufferings punctuate contentment? 'Explore yourself, Daughter. Find that magnificence within the mundane. I have made you with all care and pride that art could bestow. The science of life, you will have to discover yourself.' Father's voice reverberated through the cave. 'Your habits can't remain caged within the perks of beauty. It anyway isn't your own achievement; it's mine. Your success lies in negotiating the contrast. Go challenge your comfort, Woman, and come back with wisdom. That's the spread before you. Pick your bait, all that you can. Adjust, understand, conquer.'

'Why him?' I whispered earnestly.

'Gautam is the most visible contrast to your existence, Daughter. Your innocence to his intelligence. Your tender to his tough. Your cheerfulness to his reserve. Your beauty to his personality. Your rigidity to his flexibility …!' Father may still have had something left to say in appreciation of the sage, who was audience to the conversation but stood apart in mind and body. He was present as if he were absent. As if we were talking about someone else. As if he was no more than an obsolete, barren bark of an old tree. And this, Father insisted, was his power – to stay immune to both praise and criticism! I interrupted in protest.

'His flexibility, you said?' From the corner of my eye I looked at his lean torso, the muscles jumbled like a rope, and face as stiff and uncompromising as a corpse.

'Contrast is the origin of discomfort, my dear,'

Father advised. 'Anything that lies beyond the boundaries of knowledge causes inconvenience. Life is about conquering the contrast instead of running away from it.' He smiled. 'As much as Gautam is a contrast to you, you are an offensive contradiction to his way of life. His means are austere, while you seem soaked in luxury, fresh out of Father's cradle. Your skin with the scent of sandalwood has never passed through the ashes of a dead fire. Your demands are a threat to his practices of restraint. And yet he never protested. He allowed my verdict to fall upon him as the discretion of his destiny. He is ready to adapt with you without dishonouring his pursuits. But you stand here pleading miserably. If he isn't flexible then who else is?'

My childlike excitement gave way to a sulking depression. Father didn't notice that I had started shedding my expectations. He continued with his monologue, showering me with wisdom. Wisdom that helped me to look within Brahma's mind. Wisdom that hurt.

'The world is wary of Brahma's cave,' he

continued. 'No one is permitted to even peep inside. But you consider it home because you have full knowledge of its interiors. Step out of the zone of comfort that will limit you. Embrace the unexpected. Demolish the crust of the concealed, lavish yourself with the view of the one without a mask, and move on.'

While taking me through the rulebook of an ideal life, Brahma may have forgotten about the very basic knowledge that comes embedded in humans, effortlessly. They believe their father would protect them with all their might, that he would never let them feel unwanted. My first learning was that I was alone and all by myself. I might be my father's pride, but I was not loved nor revered. The realization strangely calmed me.

Defeated by the logic of deeds and left with no other means, I bid adieu to Brahma.

From the edge of Heaven I looked downwards. It was a steep path with scanty vegetation. Feathery clouds floated about. I tried to touch one of them and it melted away on my palm. The water smelt of lavender. I tried to wipe it off, but it wouldn't go. The wetness clung on, like tears, alluring me to not step ahead. But Gautam had already started walking ahead. I had little option left than to follow suit. It felt lonely and scary, unsure of what lay ahead. Slowly I walked, looking back repeatedly, wondering whether Father would send along one of his trusted representatives. He didn't. Opaque smoke shrouded the path behind. Nothing was visible anymore. Only the Mist followed us.

Gautam took rapid steps, driven by a strange haste to reach his destination. But I wanted to revere in the journey. The streams that went down with us, the birds and butterflies introduced themselves en route, the plants that swayed to welcome us at every corner seemed like long lost allies. They had something to tell me; I could sense that in the sprinkle of the dew, the chirrups of the passerine and the groans of the gutsy autumn winds through the leaves. They perhaps wanted to disclose the story of the past. The past that I didn't have and yet a lot had taken place before me to take mighty control of whatever happened next! I wanted to hear the mysterious music and explore the symbols left by Nature to discover those enigmatic tales. But I wasn't permitted to stop. Gautam didn't look back, nor did he enquire about my comfort. With an absurd pace he walked on, no resistance interrupting his strides. All the huge stones, the slippery moss, the misleading mushrooms, the cheerful flowers – he crossed everything with dispassionate ease. My feet were bruised. Corners of the garment warming my body ripped and entangled in the thorny bushes. My body felt weak, and the skin dry. Gautam though showed no mercy.

I wanted to know about the place where we were headed. The solitude of a seemingly dead track was as deafening as was the unreliability of the destination. But something in Gautam's unbending aloofness warned me that I wouldn't be encouraged to employ the shortcut of servicing myself on cooked grains. My learning in every aspect of life will have to be acquired through observation and experience, not through the guidance of a mentor or parental supervision. While striding through the remote and uneven terrain, more than once I looked around to spot an alternate path. A small diversion within the woods maybe, where flowers bloomed radiantly and streams fell hastily from above on a little lake with transparent water. Where rocks were friendly enough to offer a seat and the soft grass below was welcoming. Perhaps a small secluded space where the dominating mesh of powerful branches above would give way to the clear sky. The cold water of a lake with lotuses below would perhaps relax my wretched, dusty frame.

The problem with human beings is that they hallucinate what they can't attain. Their heart negotiates with the brain to carve a reality away from reality. These are called dreams. They appear and go, leaving the affected even more disappointed with their helplessness.

Not a single turn showed up anywhere. Dense forests on either side left only one path to tread upon, the one that we were on. Strange and silent. My desire to run from the sage died its natural death. Round went the sharp turns through which we travelled, every turn detaching us from

AHALYA

Heaven by some cruel conspiracy. And with every turn my memories of Heaven faded away. The time I spent roaming around freely as a soul, images of my body being carved with diligence, conversations with Brahma, my little secret with the Kalpavriksha, all kept transposing on to the deepest trench of the subconscious on which I had no control to restrict or to retrieve. I seemed to be approaching Earth like a newborn, the mind clean like a blank canvas, ready to create its own patterns with colours of life.

Gautam led me through tall mountains and solitary valleys to finally arrive at his hut. Small and dark, its door-less entrance faced the dense forest and the rear end overlooked the river. He stopped to quench his thirst and left immediately, leaving me all alone, without any information on where he was headed to or when he would return. There was no instruction on what I was expected to do, where? all I could tread or which audacious experiments I must avoid. A newborn though has her own anxiety. The tension of being a stranger in her own world, the impatience to traverse the obscure till it is thoroughly surveyed. When there is no one to formally introduce the world to her, she sets out to venture herself. She is confident of her toddler steps as much as she is hesitant. And she is at the peak of her exploration, unyielding to the risks of harm, swaying to the call of the unknown to discover whatever is tucked within the feisty suspense of nature.

I was no different. The first few hours of inertia were perhaps a preparation for the body to rove around in subdued valiance. This strange place felt unnerving and lonely. My body throbbed with a thousand complaints, unsure of whom to thrust them upon. With disdain, unable to think any further and unwilling to heed the consequences, I fell on the ground and lost myself in deep sleep. Smiling tenderly at my immature impulse, oblivious of the guile of the world, the Mist stood guarding at the doorway like a thick unyielding curtain.

3

On the banks of river Mandakini, was Gautam's ashram, his secluded hermitage. Some of his disciples lived around in huts scattered across miles. Gautam woke up before sunrise, took a bath in the river and began with his rituals, while his disciples gathered log from the forest and arranged them in a corner on the open porch. The sage swept the surroundings using huge leaves. His disciples washed the courtyard with the water he carried back from the river. Facing the east, he set up a *kunda*, the sacrificial fireplace. Before the holy fire they sat and chanted austere verses that were difficult to pronounce, yet they mouthed them with remarkable ease. Agni or fire, I learnt from the Mist, is the mouth of the Gods. It is the carrier of the oblation and acts as the messenger between human and divine, the bridge between human consciousness and the cosmic consciousness. Sacred fire converts material offerings into psychic components before they are offered to the deities, which propitiate the energies of the Gods through spiritual transformation. Every morning, the heavenly aroma of wood and wild herbs filled the air, inviting the Sun God to end his routine detachment.

From behind the Mist I peeped to witness the rhythm that bound these bizarre people bound by strict codes of conduct. No one smiled, no one blinked, no one cringed with the chilly morning breeze; they didn't even look around to observe how nature presented a unique miracle for mankind with every new sunrise. The chirrup of birds didn't disturb them; the murmur of leaves was the mundane groove of nature that they were much accustomed to. I seemed to be the only odd contrast to the entire setting. The one who looked at the world as if it were a magical collection of unpredictable ventures, as if every moment were a metaphoric disclosure of its inherent mystique. Else, everyone knew thoroughly the duty they were expected to fulfil, and like machines they exercised no deviations. Each one of them was dedicated to the mission in front, their eyes accustomed to the sacred flames with days of practising penance. After the fire sacrifice, each morning Gautam sat down with his followers, preaching them philosophy and the truth of life.

From whatever I heard and understood of Gautam's words of wisdom, the sage and his disciples were trying to unravel the paradox of time. And here I was still caught up with the transient fantasies of beauty. Their pursuits seemed more metaphysical, and my interests, earthly.

I wasn't ever invited out to join the rest of the people in the daily rituals. I wasn't formally debarred either. I wasn't ever asked a question. Since the day of my arrival Gautam didn't enter the hut even once. The fruits and vegetables he brought back were kept silently at the doorstep. He never asked whether I ate them or if they were picked up by the apes and deer that roamed around freely. He never bothered to find out whether I needed something or if he could help me with anything.

Restlessly, I walked inside the little hut. Over an ill-built framework of bamboo, hay had been wrapped clumsily and soil coated unevenly to construct a frail structure. Though it looked like the hut would fall with a mere gentle push, the establishment was tough. Who knows for how many decades it stood there, building its resilience while roughing in the sun, washing through the monsoons and enduring the winter flakes! On a particularly depressing day I tried to support my back on the inside wall, seeking reassurance and comfort, whatever little the lifeless enclosure could provide. The structure felt lumpy and coarse. Any accidental friction on the surface scratched my skin, making it bleed.

It felt at times this hut wasn't meant to be a resting place, which should relax the nerves or sooth the body. It inspired rather to stay away, to find solace somewhere else. This little uncomfortable structure was anything but a home. It was just an ill-humoured prank of offering a doomed bed which leaves the user sleep-deprived. It felt more like a prison. Just that no one here kept any vigil on the captive. Perhaps because this place had no escape!

Thoroughly offended, I inched towards the exit.

The large world outside seemed alluring from the small exit of the hut. I wanted to run around and seek a formal introduction with each of the surrounding elements. But I wasn't sure whether it would be safe, whether I was permitted to do this. When no one was watching I sneaked to the stream running down the forest to wash and to feel alive! I returned long before sunset. Within the four feeble walls of the clay hut I slept alone, terrified every time the wild beasts howled from afar. Gautam lay prostrate outside, his body rested in a deep sleep. The Mist came rushing to hug me during those fragile moments.

'Go back to sleep,' she assured, passing her long, loving fingers through my hair. I tried to hold her back, to feel protected and cared for, and buried myself in her lap. The Mist cuddled like a pad around my ears, impairing all unpleasant clamours of Nature from reaching me. Slowly restlessness faded away, anxiety disappeared and I surrendered.

While returning from my daily excursion to the stream I started collecting the clay that deposited on the banks. I wrapped it in the end of my cloth and carried it back to the hut. I applied it thick and even on the walls and on the floor. The texture changed soon, so did the rough interiors. All through the idle hours of the days and sleepless moments of the nights I kept myself engaged with this hopeless activity, somehow giving a purpose to my life as I wiped and mopped the crude surface. When I was tired to the bones and my muscles ached so badly that the resounding cry of wild boars couldn't reach me any longer, I fell into deep sleep with my clay-stained fingers.

AHALYA

Soon enough this work of recasting was also over. I was rendered jobless once again. As much as the plain, smooth walls and floor brought me the joy of renovating from ugly to beauty, equally was it frustrating. There was no one I could invite to feel the difference, to experience the change and to appreciate the transformation.

Once again, the days passed as I restlessly twirled through my meagre jurisdiction, trying to find myself an occupation, and hoping to show up significantly, to be noticed by the other living creatures that hovered around speechlessly.

After several days of watching and observing, as a prisoner within the four walls, one morning I stepped out as soon as Gautam left for his bath. Swiftly I collected the large leaves fallen on the ground and swiped the place clean. The unnecessary particles fallen on the floor were pushed leftwards to prepare the porch for the rituals. Unaccustomed hands cleaning the earth for the first time, raised some ruckus. A cloud of dust threw themselves upwards in protest; the fresh morning air felt polluted. I coughed, eyes pricked, hands dirty. I ran inside just before Gautam reappeared.

He stood there surprised for a moment, then threw the water he carried back from Mandakini. The transparent splashed all around, putting distressed particles to rest. The pollution didn't suffocate him; he seemed to adapt to it as just another mundane tantrum of Nature. For me though Gautam showed neither appreciation nor contempt. Things moved on exactly the way they did before. Unwilling to yield, I swept the ground every day before Gautam's return. Soon, he grew accustomed to it and carried on with his chores till I prepared to shock him once again. That morning I carried a half-broken pot I discovered behind the hut as I walked up to the river. With great effort I gathered as much water as I could and let it flow cautiously on the dry ground, careful that my efforts didn't invite adverse results. Swiftly, the water spread in all directions, forming thin, serpentine streams, unheeding of any regulations that I may have set. I ran after them to exert my control, ensuring that they touched every inch of the ground. I played around chasing the water, as it flowed ahead in haste; I ran forward to arrest it and bring it back to the spaces it must clean. When Gautam returned from his bath he surveyed with his usual calm; he wasn't surprised. He behaved as if he was expecting this development to follow. Simply without wasting a word, his face as apathetic as it could be, he pulled the kunda and started preparing the fire.

Thoroughly disappointed with his nonchalance I frowned. Nothing! Not a word nor an expression? No smile on the face nor scorn? The 'first time' of anything is like an important personal growth of shifting base from one step to the next higher rank. It has its own merits and expectations. Non-response is the worst insult that can be inflicted upon a harmless heart, ambitious of crushing a pattern. Disgusted, I looked at the Mist.

'Don't feel so baffled,' she tried to pacify. 'Gautam is a hermit, a recluse. He won't respond to those little things that mean so much to you. Those simple personal needs don't feature in his horizon. His world is larger, his concerns more profound. His attention is invested elsewhere.'

Dejected, I looked outside the small window of the hut. Gautam and his disciples had stepped out for their regular walk through the woods to the neighbouring villages. There they travelled from door to door, sharing words of wisdom, wishing the families well, serving the ill and feeble with therapeutic herbs, and in return were presented with fruits and vegetables. I heard these when the boys discussed an ailing villager while crushing seeds for his medication. Not that I was eager to talk to Gautam. I just needed my existence validated. The fatigue of a jobless, friendless life was depressing. Like a ghost I walked around the place, waiting for someone to acknowledge my presence. Maybe someone would stop me when I walked too deep into the forest. Perhaps someone would laugh when I lost my way. Or someone would wait at the door to chide me for staying out till so long. I was looking out for someone like me – a human being – for whom my little world wasn't an unnecessary indulgence.

But that was not to be. It was only Nature that splashed water from the stream to drench me, caressed my skin from invisible corners with gentle breeze, tickled my feet when the rowdy ingrowths haphazardly spread across my path, and the seasons brought harshness of summers, moisture-laden monsoons or the cool of winters to restore faith that I too am alive! Venturing closer to the honeybees' huge abode made them defiant. Before stepping away from their treasure retreat, I sensed that some creature on the planet could also be terrified of me. Late in the night when everything fell silent, an occasional humming of the crickets or a sudden cry of a herd of deer included me in their humdrum. And early in the morning little birds tried to peek through the tattered roof, singing songs of glory, awakening me to their tireless exhilaration. Gautam or his disciples had no time or interest. It seemed that they almost forgot that I occupied a part of the same universe. Yet I kept making small advances with each passing day, trying to change the format of my life and theirs, reminding them of me and keeping myself excited with those self-imposed insignificant targets.

I brought back seeds and stems from the forest to place them below the soil bordering the hut. Soon, red, yellow and purple flowers smiled back brightly. I planted a neem tree outside the window. It grew up fast, raising overt branches skywards; the trunk looked broad, wide and mighty. I picked up the tattered strings from the brahmins'[3] sacred thread, lying discarded and overused on the banks of Mandakini. Joining one with the other, entwining the ropes into a messy bond, I hung a hammock from the branches of the neem tree. During the evenings I sat there unmindfully, the unruly breeze titillating through my hair and bare skin.

At times I ran into the forest where the usual din of Nature sounded like the strange voices of old mortals imparting cryptic wisdom. I ignored the voices to watch the swarm of ants making

---

[3] Brahmin: The priestly class among the Hindus.

their way up the trees with extreme enthusiasm. Even a small rotten fruit on the top was enough to bind them with unflinching focus. Cocoons ruptured to release proud butterflies flaunting their elegance with every flap of wing. Wild ducks marched around and bickered noisily to demolish the calm. Startled, I attended to their baffling quacks to decipher the root of their disagreement. But before I could concentrate, the bright-eyed fawn was pulling me away, tugging at the corner of my garment. I fondled her gentle golden skin interspersed with white dots. Happily, she tagged along to give me a tour of the forest. A little pool formed by the stream falling from above, the mushy ground with deep pugmarks where scary animals traversed at night, the dangerous creeks over the soft puddles formed by fallen trunks, the holes where snakes rattled and rats bred, and the irregular bed of flowers where bees and butterflies flocked together for nectar. I plucked a few flowers to adorn the edges of the hut. I climbed up the massive trees to source fruits and leaves that grew on them; otherwise I just sat on their branches looking at the world from above. The villages far away were visible from here. Thatch-roof huts and their residents appeared tiny. But there was a touch of that very human mayhem, apparent even from this distance.

I served Gautam the fruits and edible leaves I carried back. He accepted them without a word and distributed them among his disciples. When he shared his wisdom with the followers, I often stepped out to sit with them. The Mist covered me with a colourless veil, so I remained concealed from the rest of the world. Only Gautam noticed, but he did not object. His deep voice explaining meanings of life and doctrines of philosophy dug into my brain, his interpretations of complex academic texts discussed possible deviations and exceptions. With great mastery Gautam translated for his students the occult of Ayurveda. He demonstrated the role of the ailing body in its own healing with exceptional intelligence. I absorbed his teaching with deep interest as his words opened up a new horizon for me to think and reflect upon. I had learnt all his hymns and chants by now, much faster than his disciples.

4

I included a visit to Mandakini among my regular chores. Before Gautam woke up I would have already travelled the distance and back. I used his pot to bring water for the dry porch. At those unearthly hours, when the moon still shone bright, I ventured out wearing the Mist as my shawl. Mandakini looked majestic. Flowing in vigour, she welcomed me with the eternal music of her waves flirting with the pebbles lying in her depths. The riverbank seemed encrusted in silver. As my shadow fell on the river, the water sprang up in ecstasy and dropped back like a small child attempting to run with unprepared feet. On nights when the moon observed its fortnightly leave, the fireflies came rushing in hoards to light up my path with their glowing phosphorous.

Other than the Mist, only Mandakini looked happy to have me around. The natural charm and irresistible energy was perhaps embedded within her character. As I moved closer the water came gushing to soak my feet and the cloth hanging towards the bottom. With great force it formed fragile bubbles on the surface. I tried touching the bubbles and they ruptured. I went deeper into the river, now standing knee-deep. The water stared back, waiting for me to trust more and offer myself unbarred. With a tender touch it charmed me to resign and let go of my non-existent hold over everything permanent or perishable. I bent my knees and fell on the sand for the water to run over every corner of my body and ease my restless muscles. With unpredictable strokes of her waves, Mandakini played around splashing not only on my body but also soothing my overcast mind. Within a few moments of meeting she made me feel alive and wanted! I got up to venture closer

AHALYA

and embrace the welcome more wholeheartedly. She let me slip and fall, yet held me firmly with her aqua hands girdled around my waist; her ploy would unsettle, not hurt. And then she laughed! In my desperation to seek acceptance I assumed this was special, meant exclusively for me. And yet I strongly felt that there was something brewing between the two of us. Something that indicated we had a long way to go, together. A kinship was growing.

At times she would vigorously participate in a rugged sport, bouncing me off from one bank to the other. And there were also days when she would let me float on her like a stray leaf, without a destination, bereft of a distinguished aspiration!

Perhaps Mandakini too was deprived of a human connect as much as I. Gautam and his disciples may have been as indifferent with her, as they were with me.

Years passed.

I was least aware of the changes that had started showing on my body, transforming me from a girl to a woman. Only when drops of red trickled down my limbs I reached out to my timeless companion, the Mist, frightened that I must have been devoured by some cureless ailment. Nervous and agitated I asked the Mist whether I should reach out to Gautam, asking him for some of his unfailing medication. With tender care the Mist held me close to herself and explained the wonders of a woman's body. I listened in awe. And one morning the transparent water of the Mandakini reflected an image which was starkly different from what I had seen when I had peered for the first time. My features had changed, the curves far sharper, confidence high and the physique full of suspense. Nature and its unexpected turns now failed to keep me intrigued all through the day. Some other illegitimate call occupied my dreams. It was as immoral as crossing well-defined boundaries fixed by no one, yet everyone knew of their existence. The Earth beyond the borderline felt like an inevitable stop towards my ultimate yet vague destination! I started walking towards it fearlessly.

I fantasized of a forbidden touch. I was

standing at the threshold of a mysterious gate with a broken lock. Hesitant hands dared to push it open. A flood of glittering clouds formed a colourful hammock, inviting me to shed apprehensions and embrace the untamed. I closed my eyes to receive a kind, imaginary face with strong unrelenting hands pleasuring my lean built, his passion igniting the depths of my soul. Not a single person on Earth was aware of the explosion I felt within. I floated in the joy of discovering my self, far beyond the capacity of any great teacher to analyze or interpret. I touched myself with an urgency, to unravel the miracles that a body can bring to the mind. I felt with my hands the smooth skin and beyond, exploring myself a lot more than I ever did. A gentle press or a robust stroke invoked freedom of a different kind. No other knowledge, no experience, no wisdom had ever unravelled so much about myself to me as did this blasphemous plunge into self-indulgence. My heart though still remained barren.

After those sinful night-long escapades I reached out to Mandakini in the morning. She expressed no contempt towards my adventures. With her usual delight she welcomed me in, gliding softly through my body to cleanse and prepare me for a whole new phase. Her rippling waves whispered in my ears, 'Go woman, find your world yourself. Don't stop till the happiness in your dreams merge with the reality of your life. The joy you seek deserves to be discovered.' I turned and twisted with the force of her flow, as my tense muscles cooled down after a night full of excitement. She managed to recast me back to my timid frame, to not present the self overtly before the Earth in broad daylight. Humble and withdrawn I filled water in Gautam's large vessel and walked back to his hermitage to prepare the pristine ground for his morning rituals.

The Mist stood witness to this fresh euphoria, perhaps sighing in silence as her melancholy echoed through the air. I was too absorbed in the exuberance of the moment to take note of her sudden depression warning of the turmoil in the days to follow, as does every child in ignorance of the concerns bursting inside a mother's heart.

I continued to sit through Gautam's morning preachings, albeit at a distance, afraid of the sage reading through my distractions. The Mist enveloped me to near invisibility, and Gautam, as usual, didn't pay heed to my partial presence. His voice, firm and peaceful, reached me through waves in the morning air, enriching its audience. Such is the voice of a teacher. It seeps into the mind through unseen pores and inspires intelligence. It forces you to think, observe, learn and discuss, to outgrow the dimensions of your shadow by walking towards a brighter light. For a student though that scholarly knowledge gets analyzed and interpreted through the most compelling ideological calls of their character. Gautam taught philosophy. I learnt that the entwined strength of art, science, birth, life and religion influences subscriptions to a chain of beliefs first and intimidates later with the slightest diversion. Gautam taught geography and astronomy. I learnt how naming a place or space limits it with boundaries. Gautam taught yoga, Ayurveda and human anatomy. I learnt that the human body is sensitive; it is the recipient of pleasure and pain, largely dependent on what the mind chooses for the body. It is a silent volcano waiting to erupt as the explosives accumulate within its secret sac, conspiring against time.

At times Gautam's voice suddenly felt unfamiliar. From its usual coarse and rather shrill tone it would turn deep, seemingly heavier, with more message than his spoken words could contain. It would happen at the blink of an eye, and before I could look up to inspect more it was gone. Gautam would be back again in his usual disdain, imparting lessons of life as he always did, as if nothing were ever inconsistent. But still I felt there was another character to Gautam, surpassing the repulsive image he had attached with himself. A person hiding behind his austere means, as stealthily as he can, not to cause any hindrance in the sage's usual reserve. A presence that even Gautam wasn't quite aware of.

Or maybe it was all the imagination of my idle mind frustrated in the absence of fair occupation.

One morning I was self-absorbed in my secret

pleasures on the banks of Mandakini and lost count of time. I didn't notice when the moon had travelled down the horizon. The eastern sky disowned its darkness and birds chirped in glee. I opened my sluggish eyes to the orange sun peeping above the surface of the water as the waves muddled its reflection beneath. Nearly bitten by a scorpion I sat up alarmed. My reverie was broken. Quickly I let the water cleanse the remnants of the illicit hours. I filled the pot and stepped out of the water in haste, ready to start another mundane day. Hardly had I noticed that Gautam had approached with brisk steps to take his bath. I turned and stood frozen, facing him. My body wet, hair dishevelled, fine cloth enwrapping my curves but hiding nothing, eyes bold and terrified simultaneously, I was almost bare before him. Astonished and embarrassed Gautam's routine zest slowed down even before he knew. That gross uncalculated moment of indignity slipped from his control ...

My nude being observed by a man for the first time felt adventurous. Every design of the body notoriously provoked all instincts to collapse walls and bridge the distance between us. He was the only man I had ever known! Gautam's eyes traced my body from bottom to top, their language suddenly turning savage. They stopped eventually at the joint of my eyes to read further, deeper. The indifferent gaze was suddenly engaged, trying to decipher something unimportant yet powerful. It seemed locked in the interpretation of the unexpected rather than extending a pleasant gratification. The meagre belongings fell from his hand. Bound by a cruel spell he waited motionless for a few moments. Then he turned and disappeared.

For the next few days Gautam couldn't be found anywhere.

Fearing the unknown I too did not step out of the hut. With my most guarded secret suddenly exposed, the darkness within the four walls felt like a comforting, superficial cover over a woman's immodest audacity to prioritize selfish pleasure over spiritual happiness. The porch remained uncleaned, unwashed; Gautam's disciples did the chores whenever they came, shocked with my sudden withdrawal but not uttering a word. They watered the saplings I had planted, brought back fruits for me in the evenings and placed them at the doorstep just like Gautam did. The flowers I brought back to decorate the edges of the hut dried and decayed, emanating a pungent smell, till the breeze threw them away.

Seldom did I know that boundless pleasure attracts cruel penalty. Such is the balance of life.

5

Late that evening storms from the north invaded the banks of Mandakini. Unprepared for the calamity the Mist guarded the entry of the hut, as was her usual evening ritual, while I sulked sitting in a corner. The sudden rage of Nature jostled us both. Strong winds came roaring by, threatening severe devastation. Mercilessly they pushed the Mist inside. She fell face down on the hard floor before I could rush towards her, the small opening of the hut left blatantly exposed. With no one protecting the entrance from outside either, the menace ravaged around brutally, ransacking whatever came in its way. Trapped inside I shivered in the cold. The sound of the strong iron *kunda* thumping away to a distance reverberated with the vigour, creating an intimidating rhythm of the unforeseen. Before we could decide whether the kunda needed to be reinstalled in its designated place, lest its tarnished insides corrode, the huge neem tree I had once planted with great care broke off from its trunk and fell on the ground with a terrible thud, shaking up the Earth and every kind of life thriving on it. The tree now stood like a ghost, beheaded in a brutal war. The fallen heap of leaves rustled for one last time, releasing a deep sigh and doling out a strange warning in the vicious air: *Run if you can, from everything around here. They are bringing down every shield that was meant to protect you. Soon they will get to you.*

'Who?' I screamed helplessly, unable to figure what I should stay warned of. The ghastly winds blew again in force, thunderous clouds collided with each other, obstructing any other voice to reach me. The leaves were dragged afar by the storm.

AHALYA

I trembled in the arms of the Mist. With less assurance in her dampened morale she held me tight and tried to tell me that things would settle soon. The storm damaged more, its demons dancing in fury through the forest and the river and the hermitage. As a parting note of the massacre it blew off the roof of the hut and left me drenched in unrestricted, ice-cold downpours. With barbaric force it pulled me apart me from the folds of the Mist. I tried to hold back to her in inconsolable despair – the mother who comforted me through all my pains, my longings, my adventures, my loneliness. Lightning cracked with thunder, laughing aloud like a hundred thousand evils. My mother disappeared within the layers of that cruelty.

Our separation was symbolic of the impending annihilation serving a prelude to another upcoming storm that would continue to destroy, without showing signs of devastation to the visible world. This time it would be an internal conflict where my personal choices would be in friction with imposed obligations.

Grief-stricken, I was left with myself and some meaningless drops of tears, as the world calmed down. Feeling lawlessly molested by the inhumane, my muscles ached. Ransacked inside out by every possible loss, the troubled brain claimed to retire. Fallen on the floor like a plundered traveller, I wondered what misdeed may have brought upon me such horrific punishment! Or was it Nature's wrath in response to the damage I may have caused to Gautam's abstinence? Unsheltered and orphaned I trembled, groping for answers to endless ambiguous queries till deep sleep overpowered my agony.

It wasn't a peaceful rest, but the worn-out brain pulled me into a state of suspension I wasn't ready to wake up from. Hours later I finally managed to pull myself up. My clothes still felt uncomfortable; my limbs hurt. There was brightness everywhere. I covered my eyes with a hand to block this sudden burst of light. I remained fallen hopelessly in denial of everything I had lost the night before. I refused to receive the present, the darkest I have ever been in broad daylight. Suddenly, a deep, alien voice resonated through the interfering blaze.

'Ahalya!'

Shocked, I sprang up on the ground. I didn't remember the last time someone called me by my name. I had almost forgotten that part of my identity! From behind the light emerged a strange creature looking like a human being but not exactly one. I turned myself away the sight. The ordeals seemed never-ending. I wanted to weep but was too frightened to have even the tears speak of my woes. The creature didn't seem threatening though. 'Ahalya,' I heard it calling again, the voice reassuring this time, perhaps also amused. I turned this time. Tall and lean it stood. The light that glowed like a destructive fire was now subdued. It hung behind the figure softly as does a rain-washed morning sun behind the banyan. The creature had the body of a man with four heads resting on the neck, each looking at one of the four directions. White hair and long beard. Four hands instead of the usual two, carrying a water pot, a spoon, a book, a rosary and a lotus.

'Who are you?' I asked.

'Brahma, the Father,' he beamed.

'Whose father?' I asked, unsure of the ideal question at this hour, the answer to which will put me to ease.

'Father of each and every element of this universe. Did you hear about *Brahmanda*?'

I nodded. The word had often appeared during Gautam's preaching, referring to the infinite. I remembered the mention of Lord Brahma too. Is this the same Brahma? Must be, the descriptions do match inch by inch.

'Brahmanda means Brahma's creation,' he said, startling me all over again. 'I am the creator of the cosmos. I bind it into rules and also set it free.'

Unwilling to engage in any philosophical discussion at this juncture I approached it more directly. 'Why do you have four heads? It looks unnerving.'

Brahma smiled. 'Anything that lies beyond the boundaries of knowledge causes inconvenience.'

His words this time sounded familiar, something

that I had heard before. My subconscious was chasing some obscure memory, some unidentified conversation of the past which my brain refused to register but was quite conscious of. The four-headed Brahma was speaking again. I turned to hear him out.

'My four heads are the mouths of the four Vedas. Each of my heads spurs wisdom attained from one of the holy books. One chants hymns in favour of the deities. One is for the melodious renditions to please the fire during yagnas. One chants the priestly mantras which must accompany a fire sacrifice. The other is for the incantations largely outside the scope of the yagnas. Such are the compositions of the four Vedas – Rig, Sama, Yajur, Atharva.'

I didn't understand much of what he said. But when he spoke about the fire sacrifice and yagnas it made sense. 'You are Gautam's father?' I asked, having seen Gautam performing those rituals on his iron kunda.

Brahma smiled. 'I am your father too. And that of everyone else's. Nothing can be hidden from me. The three heads that you see are the three states of consciousness – waking, dreaming and sleeping. The fourth head behind, which is not facing you at any given time but is still present, deals with your subconscious.'

'So you are God,' I uttered unmindfully. 'Why haven't I ever seen anyone worshipping you then?'

'Once birthed the Creator's relevance is over. Vishnu comes to the forefront as he is the Provider and the Sustainer. For a human being, hence, Vishnu is the deity of prominence as he sails them through the course of life.' Brahma paused and resumed soon. 'But with every passing moment of life I am acquired in the form of wisdom. I have to be invoked and aroused with patience and renewed constantly as knowledge becomes obsolete in no time unless updated with relevance to the circumstances. I appear within individuals as intellect and bring upon them good fortune if nurtured with care.'

I didn't understand well the dynamics of being God. But though I was facing the unknown, with strange ultra-human features, my fear was replaced by hope.

I fell at his feet, partly out of devotion and partly because my body was too weak to hold myself erect any longer. 'If you know everything then relieve me of the miseries that sit on me like a thorn necklace. I need to breathe again. And return the Mist, my mother, back to me.'

Brahma ignored my rants and lifted me up.

'I had given your custody to Gautam when you were too young to sail. Now that you have grown into a beautiful young woman, I believe you no longer need to be taken care of. You are now ready to provide and nourish others.' Brahma paused.

'Does that mean I can live by myself from now on?' I asked, impatience and excitement seeping through my voice. The possibility of leaving Gautam behind and starting afresh was quite a rejuvenating proposition. My heart sank with what Brahma had to say next.

'No,' he uttered, disappointing me. 'The sage had reached out to me seeking to handover the custody. Having led a life of renunciation for all these years it would have been far more tempting for him to behold you like a lover and indulge in physical pleasures, especially when you were willing to be taken. His discipline astonished me and his honesty was inspiring. Pleased with his restraints I have given him as my blessing your hand in marriage. You would be wedded soon to Gautam and will lead a conjugal life, accepting yourselves as each other's companion.'

I lacked even the strength to protest. Not that I knew perfectly what marriage meant, but Gautam wasn't a preferred companion. This development certainly wasn't the best foundation for all those imaginary pillars I hallucinated to support my dreams on. My face though may not have been as silent as I. Brahma read the pain in my expressions.

'The strength of a man lies in the strength of his character, my girl,' he reassured me. 'When illusions of sensuous beauty can't persuade a man to break the promises he made to himself and fall for his carnal instincts, know that his sense of correctness prevails even in the most dire situations. He will stand by what is right, when everything else falls apart.'

Knowing by now that Brahma's verdicts were not to be changed, I looked outside to avoid his eyes. Obviously, I wasn't convinced. This was only getting bad to worse. On the open ground beyond the window the broken trunk of the neem tree reminded of the destructions of the night. Sharp tremors passed through my veins, scaring the already anxious soul. The sight was terrible. I looked back at Brahma's affectionate face.

'What you just saw was beautiful once, my child, but it wasn't strong enough to sustain the beauty. It fell prey to a storm.' He smiled. 'External beauty is an illusion that captivates the human brain. You start thinking that an object of beauty is imperishable, invincible. The truth is there's nothing more vulnerable than beauty as it falls to the slightest provocation. It falls from its rank when something more beautiful stands before it. It falls from its confidence the moment it is described using tangible parameters. It falls from grace as time erodes its surface. Beauty isn't worthy of trust. Yet human mind is such that it chooses the beauty that appeals to the eyes over the strength that appeals to the heart.'

Brahma paused. He was trying to convince me of something that he could have forced on me. I looked up at him wondering why. He may have read my mind and continued. 'You were not born to remain trapped in the mundane. You are Brahma's daughter; your path is meant to be far more profound, your quests deeper and pursuits complicated. Break free from the chains that have held you back to the ordinary and accustomed. I am blessing your fragile aspirations with the power of permanence.'

6

I was not sure what Father meant. Long after he left, I gathered my feeble self and walked till Mandakini. I sat there on the banks, the waves touching my feet and retreating in their natural rhythm. The Mist resurfaced and sat at a distance, staring at me. Delighted with her arrival and simultaneously miffed by her unusual reserve I asked, 'What is a wedding, Mother?'

'Wedding is the spiritual union of two human beings. Keeping the fire in between you sacrifice all your individual pursuits to follow joint goals. The body, heart, mind and soul of both merge into one, and they start living like a unit. Nothing exists in isolation ever again.'

Her explanations confused me further. 'Can two people really merge their lives in a way that nothing exists in isolation? What if my personal quests don't match with my partner? Do I give them up in the fire and never think of them again? Is that even practical?'

'Your quest should be to fulfil your fantasies through your partner. Work on him, so he raises himself to your standards. Help him to see through you. And at the same time elevate yourself to understand him. There might be frictions, but don't give up. Eventually both individuals end up discovering the common purpose that binds them. That is the path which unites as well as liberates. Because it is the togetherness that helps people sustain.'

Even the Mist seemed convinced of Brahma's obnoxious arrangement. Having remained a close confidante to all my secret fantasies, how could she fall for the verdicts of Father so easily! I sulked in silence.

AHALYA

Perhaps to cheer me up the Mist brought her mouth close to my ear. 'Don't you wish to explore yourself with the man who has never been explored before?' she whispered. 'With you his body will breathe; he'll reciprocate your passion the way you want; from you he'll learn to desire. Tread with him into that journey which Gautam had never taken before. Play with him at every step; enslave him to your fantasies. Avenge him for that indifference you always complained of. Arouse him with shrewd strokes; let his restraint explode.'

Mandakini sent her relaxing breeze to fill my tensed heart with vigour as Mother tried to prepare me for a new chapter. It sounded more tormenting than exciting. But then that's probably the difference between a father and a mother! The father passes his decree and disappears into oblivion, but the mother explains to reassure, to comfort. The father's love is ambitious and the mother's, emotional.

The Mist straightened herself and came closer to echo the same thoughts passed by Father. 'You have judged Gautam with whatever your eyes have seen of him. Allow him to present himself in grandeur, the magnificence of which can reach beyond your eyes. Women are born creative. Create in him the one you have always desired.'

Preoccupied with the sudden turn of events, I didn't hear her well. I looked back at Mandakini. Calm and transparent she flowed, unconcerned with the dark dilemma troubling my mind. For long we sat together in silence, the Mist holding me close to her as I buried my head into her chest, till I heard her saying, 'I have come to bid adieu.' Shocked, I looked at her, releasing myself from the warmest comfort I had ever known. Her eyes were still as glass. 'I now have no place here. You will have to start your life with Gautam. And you will have to grow out of my shields. I can't stay put any longer to guard you from him. He must see you and experience you in your truth. So this, dear girl, is a formal goodbye.'

Startled, I sat up on the pebbles, my legs shaking. I cried. I begged. I pleaded. For the first time the Mist remained unaffected like steel. My tears could not persuade her out of her resolution. She disappeared into nothingness, leaving me all alone for the forthcoming indefinite era.

I returned to the hermitage feeling like a pauper.

Gautam was waiting there in front of the broken hut. That evening the fire was lit on the banks of Mandakini. We joined our hands to seek blessings of the setting sun. Violet and orange and red streamed across the sky like cheerful silk curtains. The gentle breeze uncannily passed through my unruly hair to set it in order. While I still stood stone-struck, hibiscuses fell from the branches and adorned my hair, the soil on the riverbank stained my feet red. Twilight faded into night. The moon gifted glitters down the darkness; they encircled my neck and wrists as pearls. Restless fireflies conspired with the twinkling stars to embellish a sequinned sheen bestowing itself like the wedding canopy. Amidst his loud chants seeking blessings from Nature and Gods, Gautam smeared vermillion in the parting of my hair. With his divine mantras he invoked the Gods to seek their blessings. Jasmines and marigolds showered from above along with drops of dew as the consent of the cosmos in favour of this untoward match. I watched the sacrificial fire rising as high as it could, filling the air with its blissful aroma.

I wondered if the flames reached anyone above, in Heaven, who was as shaken up with this strange union as much as I. Was this supposed to be the beginning of happiness or the end of it all?

Back at the bereft hut Gautam arranged for stems and leaves and straw to build the roof. I had carried back the gifts of Heaven while walking away from Mandakini. Over the hay of the roof the marigolds and jasmines were placed in thin lines like pins that held the stacks in place. The celestial flowers promised to never decay, nor fall from their place, unless displaced by the beholders. Their fragrance penetrated the rough of the thatched roof to enter the hut spreading warmth and cheer. Little birds awakened by our humdrum flew around restlessly, singing songs of morning around midnight, waiting for us to finally settle and let the rest of the world fall back into slumber.

I washed the floor and the ground hoping to sweep away the ruckus from the night before. Decayed leaves and fruits with hours of negligence were pushed aside. The *kunda* was installed back to its place. Clay and sand put together were smeared to mend the broken corners of the walls. Crushing together granite, pumice and limestone, I started making lovely designs on the ground and on the walls of the hut. Designs of a large, beautiful tree and a bounteous river, pebbles and birds, and the moon. In illustrative codes I wrote down the songs I often hummed with the Mist.

I decorated the outer edges of the hut with little purple and red flowers plucked from nearby bushes. A pot of water was neatly placed at a corner, inside. The rugged mat on which Gautam slept was cleaned and polished and tucked at one side of the clay wall. Once Gautam tied the roof, I hung colourful leaves at its ends. Fireflies flocked on them, the phosphorous on their backs shining bright to welcome the residents of the restored hut.

Only the uprooted trunk of the neem tree in the backyard could not be mended.

None of these chores were new to me. The only difference perhaps was that earlier I merely engaged myself. Now I was trying to build a home. Near the exit and on the window at the rear end, I drew the swastika to mark an auspicious start. No one taught me these. But I believe *grihastha*[4] is such a stage when a lot of worldly customs come naturally and following them feels sacrosanct. I happily drew the lines of the Surya[5] symbol first, seeking prosperity for the house. But while drawing the counter-clockwise *sauvastika*,[6]

---

[4] The **four** stages of life as per Hindu texts are Brahmacharya (student), Grihastha (householder), Vanaprastha (retired) and Sannyasa (renunciate).

[5] Swastika is the symbol of Surya when arms are pointed clockwise, denoting prosperity and good luck.

[6] **Sauvastika** is like the Swastika, but here hands point counter-clockwise, symbolizing night or the tantric aspects of Kali.

symbolizing the occult energies of the mystic, my hands trembled.

That night Gautam entered the hut.

7

I was standing by the window remembering the Mist and the bygone days. After marriage when women leave behind their trusted shelters to start a conjugal life with their husbands, they mourn the separation, while their hearts are thrilled with the adventurous possibilities of a new beginning. I had been abandoned by my kin even before I was formally wedded. Hope or happiness, there was none. I wondered where would the Mist be and how her life was shaping out without me. Just then I heard footsteps approaching from behind. Unaccustomed to any third presence on this side of the door, I turned with shock. Gautam stood there with his eyes fixed on me. It took me a while to figure out why he had crossed the threshold voluntarily. Oh, the duties of a new bride! Slowly and unwillingly I walked towards him.

His presence wasn't the longing of a lover nor the domination of a man. He didn't bring with him the possessiveness of a husband either. Standing before me was the recluse of a sage who needed to get done with a task. He looked neither nervous nor composed. He wasn't delightful or pensive. He was impassive, far more than I was distant. It seemed this night would not affect any aspect of his being. Nothing would change in his life or in his mind. The learned who possessed the wisdom of the seven worlds didn't know much about the needs of the body!

Gautam placed his hand, rough like sand, on the right of my bare shoulder. The soft skin was confused at the abrasion by stiff fingers. That was the least of his concern though. I scowled. His eyes didn't smile, attitude rigid, personality consistent as if this were no different than touching yet another ailing woman waiting to be cured. As if her yearning to be desired, to be loved, was a cancerous ailment which must be uprooted before it spread through the body like wildfire. Gautam pushed me downwards on the floor with force. Being enslaved to a life of moderation, his hands were unfamiliar with the ploys of this act. He approached like a novice, perhaps even frightened of losing his cherished chastity to the forced erotic engagement. Bony ribs bulged out of his chest like the stubborn frames of an abandoned building. Veins erect, spread unevenly on his arms, he breathed with unusual disdain to fulfil his obligation in acceptance of our new relationship.

The softness of a woman's body didn't prompt him to use his toughness with care. Pleasure was sin for him. On the irregular ground my pale shape wriggled under him. The burden of his body felt like severe discomfort. My skin bruised, flesh hurt. I wanted to throw him aside and rush out of the hut. But it was too late by then; Gautam was already bursting with energy and his strength rendered me immobile. Oblivious of the awkwardness he pushed and pulled my torso to suit his conveniences. He touched nothing. Only some distraught parts of our body collided in desperate shamelessness, bereaving ourselves of some intimate personal possessions that were now meant to be naked and shared. I clutched the uneven ground in despair, my grip searching for a grasp of relief. An extreme shot of pain seethed through.

I shrieked in horror, praying for the curse to get over.

When Gautam withdrew I looked at him fiercely. He panted in anguish like a hackneyed old man who had just offloaded his liabilities but was not feeling any lighter. Condemn in my eyes had questioned a man's virility and a husband's candour. Karma was too cruel to let go of him. It had afflicted him further, charging him of criminal assault, the pressure of which was unbearable for both. He seemed drained and defeated, as much as I was distressed. His eyes were sad and apologetic, unlike the recluse I had known him to be. As if he would erase the hour we just left behind if he could. As if the suffering that my face made no attempts to hide wasn't something he intended. As if he shared my agony much more than what we shared to consummate the strained unison between two disparate individuals. With remorse on his face and reluctance in his body, he gathered himself and left the hut.

The night was awful.

Some sleepless hours later when I came out of the hut to start my usual chores, Gautam lay wide awake, looking up at the clear sky. He saw me picking up his pot and limping away towards Mandakini, hoping to dissolve the lingering pain in the cold water. A few steps ahead I turned. Gautam was now seated up, supporting his back against the wall of the hut. His eyes were robbed of their lustre, the vigour of his being drowned in repentance. God knows what answers he was seeking from the vast nothingness above. His eyes stretched far and wide, perhaps in anticipation of an opportunity to explain himself to the all-absorbing pristine sky, only to come back humiliated – shielded by none and disowned by all. The night before had cost us my faith and his confidence. He was fallen, resigned, obligated with the helpless unhappiness of two souls. I could still seek refuge in the other interests I nurtured. I could disengage myself from my miseries and look beyond. I could bare my heart without holding back. But having practised detachment all his life, the hermit was suddenly left clueless. The lack of control, the inability to orchestrate the moments the way they should ideally be and the rejection apparent in my expressions had hurt his pride. As much as the scars on my body felt insulting, equally was he scathed with humiliation. For a split second I felt sorry for him.

At the river I bent to fill the pot. The reflection ridiculed back. The same banks that had witnessed my wild adventures now recoiled with sarcasm. The breeze that once echoed sultry ballads in the open voiced the sadist dejection of the hour. Why did I invite this disgrace upon me? Because Brahma said so? Because the Mist tried to convince? Or was it because my faith was burnt to ashes after a fateful night and my frightened heart was searching for a protector? In the inherent haste to settle myself, I may not have considered that internal destruction is far more devastating than external threats. The heart is far more sensitive than the mind. The directives of life are far more complex than Gautam's principles or my whims. In my battle with unnerving insecurities I may have given up the reins of my rhythm to some unqualified relationship which ruined more than it resolved.

So, is this all about life? My life? I dared not ask. But both Gautam and I were lonelier with each other than we were before pronouncing our matrimonial vows. Both of us were perhaps disappointed with ourselves far more than our decree to condemn each other. Gautam, for doing things the way he did, unstoppable even when my discomfort showed candidly. And I, for putting myself through it without protest.

I looked back at the image in the water.

'He is alien to the generosities of the body just like you are unaware of the mystic of life. Gautam is trying to conquer life, while you want to embrace it. Go, barter with him the philosophies of two disproportionate goals. Walk the path to the source of his strength all through the day. Evoke him into the groove of alluring nights when the moon has risen. Submit when his faculty is at its prominence, control when his powers are dormant. Why barely give and take when you can actually transact?' The image whispered back a shrewd advice. 'Adapt to his means. Allow the minds to come closer. And then lead him to pleasure you. Else, even if he softens from his austere ruggedness, your bodies won't respond to each other until the hearts connect.'

A notorious ripple came rushing to shatter the reflection into several layers of water, interfering with the conversation mercilessly. Unmindfully, I balanced the pot on my waist while walking back towards the hermitage, the anxious brain still debating the uncertain path I was preparing to tread on. So engrossed was I in attending to the dilemma of my heart and the sore between my legs that I almost collided with Gautam on the narrow path that led to his ashram. He was walking towards Mandakini to start his morning. The unintentional encounter spilt unruly water on him. Startled, he stood apart, as did I. A few moments of awkwardness followed, none of us driven to bridge the cold, unfriendly aversion. I found Gautam staring at me, silently inspecting the bruises I had carried over since last night. In haste I turned to leave. Strong hands reached out before I could fathom what was in store. They disarmed me of the pot, heavy with water. He walked till his porch in fast strides, put the pot down on the ground and left immediately. I watched him from behind till he was no longer visible. With the spine erect he walked with strength, never looking back to acknowledge my gratitude towards this sudden display of kindness.

The naughty winds whispered in my ears that something had started changing even before I had invested my efforts. The force of a woman's invincible resilience had started spreading its maya in colourful clouds, under the influence of which Gautam's adamant resolve had started sinking already, as should every man's before his wife.

8

This morning when Gautam pulled the *kunda* to invoke holy fire in the presence of his disciples, I quietly walked out of the hut to take my rightful seat beside him. They must have been shocked by my unpreambled boldness, but I ignored the disapproval. The disciples exchanged quick glances. Gautam stiffened for a few moments and resumed as if nothing was unusual. My subtle dominance was the beginning of my glory. One terrible night had taught me that unless I dictated the terms, my being and my status would always be compromised. My proximity to Gautam and distance from the others signalled a non-negotiable superiority. Obedience and respect, I was meant to command, as much as Gautam deserved them. Hair tied neatly behind, clothes arranged in order, forehead smeared with vermillion, I bowed with others before the holy fire, permanently sealing my supremacy for the days to follow.

They gathered again for the hermit's discourse. He poured his wisdom on philosophy and life and human beings. With firm composure I maintained myself beside Gautam, attending to his knowledge with interest.

'God and Devil are not the opposite of each other,' he explained. 'God is neutral; he never takes sides. Devil is indifferent; he isn't bothered by the impact of his deeds or others.' Scriptures have humanized both God and Devil. The human incarnation of God is the Deva and the human incarnation of Devil is the Asura. Ancient philosophy believes that no one can be completely neutral or completely indifferent. Hence, humans can never be raised as God or reduced to Devil, both of whom are supposed to be a rigid force, omnipresent and sovereign.' As Gautam discussed complicated theories, he looked at me like he did towards others, unknowingly granting me the acceptance of being one of them, as inseparable as everyone else. With unflinching eyes, I may have learnt a little more about the sage, and about myself, as I absorbed his doctrines.

Perhaps no one had outcast me in the past when I stayed inside the hut or veiled behind the Mist. I was unattended because I never brought down my own walls to stand in the open and be found.

Soon it was time for them to pay customary visits to the faraway villages. Gautam packed the herbs and mixtures he had prepared in a large piece of cloth and hung it over his shoulder. Just as he was about to leave, I blocked his way. Surprised, and somewhat miffed with the interruption, he looked at me. The corner of my sari tied resolutely around my waist, an unfailing enthusiasm in my eye and the newly acquired rhythm of my foot declared with adamant courage that I was ready to walk with him. Gautam's expressions softened.

'It is too far. You can't come with us.' He tried to reason. He walked a few steps and knew that I was following him.

'We walk in speed. We don't have the luxury of pacing down since we have to attend to many villagers. And we have to reach out to all of them. We can't stop to rest in between. The path would be impassable.' He discouraged me. But I hadn't stepped forward to be dissuaded. Frustrated with my obstinacy, he grunted in exasperation.

'Don't follow me here, Lady. You are too tender for this journey. This is a difficult path.' He confirmed once again.

I smiled this time. 'I had walked with you from the steep mountains all the way to this hermitage, Sage! You were impatient to walk back to your holy pursuits then, while my toddler steps were trailing behind with great distress. You had never waited to ask if I needed assistance. I grew up with each new step ahead, learning the rules of the journey all by my own. What difficult path are you threatening me of now?' I asked softly.

Startled with my candid throwback, but not

ready to give up yet, Gautam now turned and faced me.

'The Earth is full of sufferings,' he said with empathy. 'Men and women here pass through many hardships, which reflect on their bodies and minds. They battle diseases, negotiate interpersonal complications, get driven by materialistic pursuits which bring misery when possessed. They are the prisoners of time, enslaved by the ephemeral cast that sits in layers over their soul.' He hesitated before pronouncing the next. 'You carry yourself with timeless elegance because you are blessed by Brahma. Time can't scorch your skin. You heal faster than others. Pangs of suffering can only touch you with temporary influence. For the world out there, it is a never-ending saga. Their minds suffer more than the bodies, resisting the muscles from recovering. Even when their body cures the mind can't forget the origin of pain, thus keeping it artificially alive. That's not something you have seen before, not something you would quite understand, not something you would like to go through.'

Never had Gautam elaborated to me, or anyone else, in such detail. His disciples followed his commands without protest. The sage was far from realizing that he had started renegotiating his own rules, falling into my terms like a decayed leaf swerving from its branch by a sudden gush of wind. Quietly, my heart smiled.

'I want to,' I declared with thrust. 'I wish to know, learn, understand. Sage, you are servicing them every day with your medication and advice. You offer unfailing treatments for their body. You rehabilitate their lost faith with your intelligence. I might not be as skilful, but I can nurse. I can touch with tenderness. I can be the mother, the sister, the friend, the daughter. You must be their inspiration. I can be their companion and confidante, comforting their angst. You can mend their nerves and I will tend to their hearts.'

'The path is barren and merciless. You will hurt your feet.' Gautam passed his last argument, though his face carried a natural delight. He seemed pleased with my dedication.

A naughty smile touched my lips. 'If I do, your

herbs will finally find some employment back home.'

So together we travelled.

Gautam and his disciples walked with speed. I paced behind them in order to remain in relevance. I tumbled over the slippery stones. Canopy of stubborn trees had us bend over them to pass. Familiar to this uneven, rigorous route Gautam's feet fell on the friendly ground that made his travel less demanding. Maybe the path knew him. It spread before him cordially, welcoming him as a friend does to another. The same path posed unceremonious obstacles for me, unbending and uncourteous towards my allegiance. I slipped on puddles; my waist pained. The blazing sun had conspired to dehydrate the world. Just out of a restricted shelter of four walls and a roof, I seemed to be his recent muse. Humidity joined hands with the heat. Perspiration made it worse; my skin was wet and the cloth near the neck drenched. Fallen branches of trees abruptly hindered progress. Uninvited cacti scattered about tattered the corners of my cloth. Slimy mushrooms greased under the unaccustomed feet. By the time we reached the village my heart had sunk. Yet I put up a brave face to pursue the vision that had brought me here.

The villagers were surprised to find a woman accompanying their healers. They frowned with unspoken displeasure.

'Who is she?' whispered one, forgetting all about the ailment he had come whimpering with.

On being informed, an old lady condemned. 'She walked with men all through the forest? How could she let go of her modesty? Such a shame!'

'Doesn't she have work at home? Which woman follows a man wherever he goes? Why is she trying to be a man?' gossiped another.

A murmur flowed in from another corner, from a young, excited farmer. 'She looks more like a seductress than the aide of a brahmin. I can't wait to fall ill now and have her hands all over me.' I cringed, while his friends patted him for having cracked the most amusing joke.

AHALYA

'Poor hermit.' This one attacked Gautam, the one who came to them from afar, caring for their health and well-being. 'Neither can he use her nor can he shed her. Look how he is busy in his own world, oblivious of what his wife is up to.' Their banter dissolved in chuckles.

I heard it all. It hurt. More than my bruised feet, the clothes tattered by cacti considerably baring the bottom of my legs mattered to them. And here I was to help them heal! But such was the politics of the workplace. Most of the people were thankless and cruel. In my courage to explore and zeal to learn they found the seed of their personal failures. Or maybe they needed a soft target to dump their frustrations on. Soon keeping their fantasies flowing became an unspoken part of my task. My presence was their escape from the mundane abuse of life. As much as they condemned my enterprising move to accompany my husband, in their hearts they looked forward to my presence. A brief eye contact, a gentle smile at the corner of the lips, a brush of air as I crossed them kept their pulses roaring. Fantasizing was their first-ever diversion from an idealist living against prohibited territories. As I touched to relieve their pains and dress their wounds, their bitterness drowned in the need to be nursed.

The only person happy to see me there was another woman, heavily pregnant with her first child. She served me water. As I returned the pot her eyes shined.

'Wait till you feel the beats of a baby inside you,' she mumbled into my ears. 'The husband would only pour his juices to be reshaped into a new life. But when the first signs of motherhood come alive, you will know the dynamics of the Earth like no wisdom can ever share. This is a science that men are still groping to learn more about; and this is one knowledge the depth of which is embedded inside the woman's uterus.' From the corner of her eyes she looked at Gautam and then back at me. Excitement flitted through the thrill of her eyes. I knew what she meant.

'Who is a mother?' I asked unmindfully, the strange question emerging from some corner of the unknown, my ignorance putting her to splits. But she didn't turn me away.

'Mother is the force that transforms energy. She is the steady host for the fidgety structureless future. She is the dream and also the destiny. She is the reason and the consequence. When water falls on the rock it serves none. But the same water stored in a container quenches thirst, it washes and it cleans too. The mother is that container who offers the holy base for the father to liberate himself of his overwhelming burden. She takes upon herself the load of a lifetime, birthing a new life, and sharing with it her intellectual and metabolic strength. She is the Creator who can confront Brahma. She is the Sustainer who can challenge Vishnu. And she is the Destroyer who can foresee such evils that Shiva may not.'

The effect of her words didn't end where they stopped. The expressions twisted and turned within my heart, trying to locate the depth of a relationship I had just been made aware of. It reminded me of the Mist, yet also exposed horizons where the Mist couldn't reach. An urge was building up within me to explore this, but I didn't know where to begin. I went back to the biggest source of knowledge that I had access to and submitted myself with an unexplained yearning to acquire.

9

Soon, I was learning about the human anatomy all over again. Pleasure of the body and feelings of the mind were what I had learnt by myself. To understand the pains, I needed guidance. Gautam explained the complexity of the skeletal structure and the mechanism of flesh, muscles and the skin that sat on it. He took me through the nature of illnesses that invaded bodies and their remedial herbs. He elaborated on the scientific contents of the plants and their extracts, and how they worked in curing wounds. Different parts of the body had their own specific complaints and needed to be treated in isolation, keeping in mind that the treatment should least affect the rest of the system. Every day Gautam would question the habits of those who sought help from him, to understand their lifestyle. He advised them to change their means if their bodies objected to their current practices. I observed his methods with keen interest and picked up on them swiftly; I came across to be a quick learner.

After treating the adults Gautam moved on to teach the children about the virtues of life. This routine would alter only if there was a birth or death or a wedding scheduled to occur in the village. Matching the auspicious time then, he would offer prayers before the Gods on behalf of the families to seek the well-being of one and all.

By the time we returned after my first day I walked inside the hut like a lifeless spirit and collapsed on the floor.

When I woke up the next morning my feet felt as fresh as any other day. The bruises had healed and the pain had subsided. My natural energy was restored. The tiny lamp placed at a corner of the room flickered light and released a therapeutic fragrance of turmeric, cinnamon and sandalwood. Who must have burnt this curative lamp while I was asleep? Gautam? The tender act of care and compassion touched my heart. I breathed in deep to inhale the luxury of the aroma. *Did he enter the hut last night?* I wondered. *After placing the herbs on the lamp did he leave immediately or did he wait?*

Unknowingly, the hermit had started warming up to me. We were connecting, slowly. The moment I engaged with his work we were bound by a common purpose. His system had started registering my presence around him more as a family and less as a stranger. The mind can bring two people closer into a bond that even two naked bodies cannot inspire! I smiled, accepting this to be the most pleasant gesture Gautam had afforded till now. This little move of affection filled me with renewed energy. With a spring in my steps I walked out of the hut, humming a gentle tune as I proceeded towards Mandakini. Gautam was right. Brahma had created me with such ingredients that my pains didn't last. Both my body and mind had this strange capacity to wake up to happiness after the darkest of nights. Seeds of delight were sown somewhere deep inside; they prevented the bitter to sustain and breed. The values that make me Ahalya. Else, how could my skin forgive Gautam so easily?

The loud-mouth breeze poked me from some unseen corner. 'That, my dear, is the essence of womanhood. The woman forgives. The ones that cause them pain, the ones that wreck their peace, the ones who are harsh and merciless, those who suppress their voices forcefully are all belittled by the woman's power to pardon.' It rustled around my ears. 'The woman is like the vigour of water. You place a rock in her way, she'll splash on it. If the rock is immovable, she'll laugh silently at its unbending contempt and make way around it without meddling with the pompous arrogance.'

I tried to ignore the unwelcome wisdom at my moment of exhilaration. The heedless breeze still hurled at me its divine forecast. 'You are the genesis of womanhood, Ahalya. Your focus, your struggles, will not only represent the spirit of women, but your pleasant spell will also fall upon men. Every living being blessed by Ahalya will learn to forgive, to nurture, to find their demure way through the toughest of barriers, to approach the world with determination and poise. Their life force will be protected and fed by inbuilt delight even in the face of extreme misfortune.' The breeze swirled away.

I concentrated back on my journey with Gautam. An enchanting path was to unfold for both of us as I prepared to remould him from a sage into a seeker.

Few days passed with the new routine I had set out for ourselves. The forest that felt so difficult and never-ending on the first day had now started making amends with me. It got friendly with little wildflowers and bees and butterflies hanging around. They warned me of the mushrooms and cacti strewn on the uneven ground. Cuckoos sang, teasing me of my buoyancy. The canopy of trees sheltered me from the scorching sun rather than engulfing me in a scary, dark web. While walking ahead steadily, leading his disciples towards their destination, Gautam would stealthily look behind when no one was watching to inspect whether I was following in spite of all the inconvenience. He ensured his glance was swift enough to never meet my eye. In return I kept myself engaged with other silly elements of the journey to never make him conscious with the realization that I adored his concern. An unspoken game had started between the unconventional spouses as Nature applied its own magic to connect two conflicted souls with contradicting priorities. Gautam's pace was slowing down with each passing day to reduce the distance between us. We both walked the same path with two different goals – Gautam's to reach the destination and mine to soak in the beauty of the journey. The sage didn't know when he had started drifting from his resolve to adapt to my way of living.

I noticed the remoulding of his character but knew better than pointing it out. He would now surprise me by pulling down branches of tall trees from which I'd wish to pluck flowers. During monsoons when everyone had large lotus leaves to cover themselves with, Gautam would pass me one, startling me with the realization that he had cared to carry an additional leaf! When the beautiful doe rubbed its head against my soft skin in sheer delight, the sage would watch affectionately its child-like demands instead of frowning at the waste of time. Each time the rustling of a snake scared me, he would distract the reptile away from my path. Gautam was increasingly becoming a *grihastha*, having set a foot forward from a hermitage to home!

The villagers soon began sharing their concerns and happiness with me as I applied a healing touch to their bodies. They blamed others for things they couldn't change. When someone brought home a pretty bride, they gathered to find her flaws. Rains during the growing season brought them cheer. The elderly spoke aloud so their daughters-in-law clearly heard how badly they had been waiting for a grandchild. Little ones complained of being bullied by playmates or their humble wood-and-clay toys being snatched away. Adolescents enquired stealthily, how was it to have a hermit as a husband! Young unmarried girls ran around after their pet goats and cows, inviting the wrath of their inconvenienced guardians. Following a death, they mourned and spoke of memories, even if they never empathized with the person when he was alive.

I listened to everything, seldom offering any judgement. As my hands, now expert with most of the procedures, serviced the sufferings of their ailing bodies, my silence interpreted as consent humoured their woes. I blended a woman's understanding of the worldly conventions with Gautam's idealistic practices to make myself available to their kinship and yet remained detached to the extent that I could to maintain objectivity in their complaints against each other.

Those who once spoke ill of me now fantasized about me; those who wondered if my courage could corrupt their women and expressed deep agony against my threatening challenge to take over the man's space had now forgotten that I had once come across as a detestable change imposed on their system without a single warning. No longer did they search for erotic pleasure when I touched. My therapy, rather, put them to sleep as a mother's lap does to her child.

10

I don't know when and how I too started making an instinctive effort to drift closer to the sage.

I stayed awake till late in the evenings watching Gautam write. Maybe he documented his sermons; perhaps he poured his imaginations through literature. Extracts from dark leaves diluted with water and thickened with oil made for orange ink. On the pale barks peeled out fresh from the tree trunks he wrote with a quill, with such concentration that his soul rested where his nib touched the brittle wood pulp. Narrow and small, his writing was conservative. He tried to fit in as many of his thoughts on a single pulp, perhaps to avoid wastage. As a writer he didn't seem as introvert as he appeared otherwise. He wrote with aggression, expressing himself with unwavering attention as if something will slip out of his authorly plates if he didn't fill them immediately or faltered in compiling his chronicles.

I lay quietly in the darkness of the hut as Gautam prepared his voracious script, oblivious of the pair of eyes that watched his every move. A little lamp flickered before him. His ribs rose and fell in the silent excitement of creation. He looked happily possessed within the realms of his own world. Bellows of elephants and footsteps of wild boars not too far away posed no threat to the grip on the quill. The bony wrist, stable on the willow plank acting as his writing desk, made no attempts to adjust the hair flowing on his back. The night breeze passed through his mane and blew unbarred to touch me. It carried with it the eloquent smell of his body.

Why did it send shivers down my spine? The thought made me sit up abruptly and I could not sleep for the rest of the night.

AHALYA

On one such evening I made my presence felt. After a heavy shower in the evening the overcast sky had just started to clear out. Dense, smoky clouds made way for a faint, arched moon. The air filled with the fragrance of moist soil mixed with fallen jasmines. In the dark of the night the ghostly rain-washed trees released their deepest sighs, the longing for a companion to possess and feel possessed by. I sprang up on the cold floor, desiring to demolish some invisible cage that restricted my flight. I felt my body awaken, not to the fantasies experienced on the banks of Mandakini but to passionate demands of a forlorn shelter. The garment fell from one of my shoulders to the ground; on the other shoulder it latched on clumsily.

I dragged myself till the entrance of the hut and waited. Gautam heard my footsteps with passive indifference. But the quill fell from his hand and his attention severely interrupted when he looked up. Bewildered eyes took a while to register the call of the moment. They stood fixed on mine, then slowly travelled downwards to my bare shoulder and arm on the right, all the way till my waist where the end of the sari was firmly fastened with multiple loops without adding any significant volume in the diameter. He looked back at me; the summon of this evening was too intense to avoid. The lotus leaf that held the ink fell with utter carelessness, instantly staining the ground and his cloth. The pulp on which he wrote shoved aside by itself to make way for the obvious adventure to follow. Roaring monsoon winds promised to spice up the evening with undisciplined, unmasked deviance.

Leaving the meagre treasure on the ground, the sage stood up. His ribs heaved and fell back, tempted to explore the unpretentious attraction, yet hesitantly held back to the memories of a terrible not-so-distant past. My lips curved sensuously at its corners to assure that memories were meant to be discarded for each new hour that inched towards progress. Our relationship was ready to kill the stagnation that settled after an unfortunate encounter and move on to explore further. This time though the wand of control would be with me!

My confidence must have shone brighter than the diffidence of the hermit. I could see his dilemma dissolving into thin air as his muscles thickened, preparing to approach and let loose. The lamp spreading the aroma of sandalwood and turmeric flickered seductively. I released the cinnamon stem that held my hair into a stiff bun; black waves came lashing down to cover the skin that lay bare till a while back. I looked away.

Tormented by the foreplay of cover and exposure, Gautam took restless steps forward. Slowly I retreated backwards; his tense advances caught up with mine in no time. Rigid hands pressed roughly on my shoulders. Prepared for his conservative means I playfully released myself from his offensive touch and guided him towards my waist instead, helping him to unbind the numerous layers of fabric. Slightly, I let my fingers slide through his, engaging his palm softly. With the other hand I brought him to feel my tender skin. For the first time perhaps the hermit came to terms with the frame of a woman, which wasn't the same as his iron *kunda* or the stones used to secrete remedial extracts from seeds. His fingers worked upwards with warmth as our walls dropped and I prepared to trust him, once again.

It was much humane this time. Eventually, Gautam seemed prepared to let go of the stubborn masculine strength to treat himself and me with compassion and longing. I wasn't ravaged so brutally like before. Pleasure was still a distant horizon, but Gautam had started treading the path. His touch had started changing from a difficult grip to a soft caress. He no longer felt interrupted by my presence around him.

With every passing hour I was falling into his routine and he into mine. I tried to engage him in conversations. He spoke less, but he listened. He lent a patient ear to my verbose as I narrated to him my interactions with the bees, the butterflies and the deer while walking with them to the villages in the morning. The bees brought me flowers after sucking nectar from them; the butterflies splashed colours on me. I showed my collection to Gautam with child-like glee. His idea of acquiring was about qualities that can't be possessed because sharing them enhanced their worth. Here I was picking up tangible assets of my own which could be stored, resulting in attachment and creating memories. Gautam didn't object even though I had deflected from his strict philosophies. With affection he watched me demonstrate how the doe had taught me to walk gently even while walking in speed, so my footsteps wouldn't trouble the fallen leaves or scare away other forms of life. He never asked what good my useless properties will fetch in our humble lives, nor was I bent upon pursuing life for a defined reason.

Gautam and I finally felt inducted into each other.

Often late in the evenings I sat down carelessly on the porch of our little hut. The night sky would be glittered with stars spread haphazardly as far as the eyes could reach. I stared at them pondering what secret they held in those tiny blinking lights. Gautam occupied the space beside me soon after, looking up at the same wonders of the cosmos. He told me about his wish to reach the stars when he would be free from the perishable body that limited him within the scope of the Earth. He started explaining the magic of galaxies and constellations, the geography of their formation and the science behind their evolution. With great attention I received every education, only to interpret it later with fictional imageries of literature. Literature had answers that science didn't. I didn't document a thing. But the wandering mind travelled beyond boundaries, discovering the conflict in available information and filling the voids with literary imagination.

These thoughts lingered till a touch on my back brought me back to reality. With a spark in his eyes Gautam would entice me towards the stars that waited for us on the Earth. I would turn towards him and place my body seductively on his lap. Our nights had now picked up the new ritual. The willow plank lay abandoned as his interests of the hour had significantly diverted.

He lowered himself towards me, while his legs stretched outwards to accommodate my spread on his lean frame. Before his mouth could touch, I caught hold of his hair and pulled him away from me under the pretext of tying his unruly hair behind. I sat up to take control over his bewilderness, while my chin faintly touched his hairline and his exhale heated up my neck. I felt his heartbeat rise and the pulse shoot as his eyes travelled impatiently all over my body, begging to be presented with the potion he had been addicted to of late. I kept him waiting, teasing and touching mischievously but unwilling to give in. Gautam was at a loss of his wits. He had always known how to command but wasn't used to the art of pleading. My terms though were not ready to budge nor compromise. And the target seemed not too far from my grasp.

Driven by boundless passion he aggressively tried to pin me down on the ground. Prepared for the coherent roughness of the inexperienced, I playfully escaped from his grip each time, only to offer myself again right from the beginning.

Just like a snake tames only after spitting venom a thousand times at its churner, Gautam's rowdiness eventually bowed to my rebellion as I silently trained him into sophistication.

11

In the morning Gautam taught me the ways and means of the colossal world, his doctrines encompassing the philosophy of life. At night I brought his intellectual self back home from the wandering vastness, grounding him with exotic revelations concerning the body and the mind. Slowly he gave up on his austere ways and started finding his own path through the labyrinth. His passion was now less reclusive and his approach less savage. He started discovering the technique of touch and the delight of togetherness, instead of brutal plundering my youthful abundance. For successive nights to follow the cosmos would witness us spending increasing hours, discovering each other in the dark, trying to understand and remould into the designs that pleasured without pretence.

In the mornings too I kept him conscious of my presence. On my way back from the banks of Mandakini my right arm brushed against his left. I blew on his hair at unexpected moments to let the strands stray and then settle. He looked up and went back to his job. When no one watched I let a corner of my cloth touch his back. He stopped for a while registering these signals and moved on. I hid his *kunda*, misplaced his writing plank, moistened his thin shawl on hot summer days. Gautam ignored my misconduct with affection. I threw berries at him from behind when he walked. Without a word he would pick them, rub their skin against the cloth he draped over himself and put them inside his mouth. At times when he serviced the villagers, I ignored the chatter of the women and stared at him, unblinkingly. Visibly discomforted he glanced back with disapproval, but his eyes appeared amused.

Gautam was finally evolving from a hermit to a husband!

The next full moon was auspicious. The brahmins gathered for a celebratory worship. People from far-off villages arrived with fruits and other homemade delicacies prepared with care and solemn piety. The rich ones brought new clothes. As per tradition the offerings made to the Lord subsequently grace the collections of the priest. Gautam gave away most of the gifts at the end of the ceremony. Only one sari, its fine threads evenly interlocked, he saved for me. The bright yellow and its borders stained with beetroot violet made for a ravishing contrast. Who knows whether it was his unmindful choice over other sky-blues or grass-greens, or whether he kept it aside among the rest because the colours wrecked his fantasies as much as they did mine!

I heard the participants attending the ceremony discuss the fascinating story behind this exquisite piece. They said, the mustard yarn weaved with complicated entwines had come from a lunatic merchant who travelled all the way from the land of Mithila. His family was famous for weaving outstanding patterns with silk threads across generations. His repute had spread far and wide, and soon he became the chief supplier of clothes to the royal palace of Mithila, where queens and princesses held his fabrics in high regard. On one dark night the merchant had a dream that approximately sixty thousand years later a newborn girl child would be discovered in the furrows of a ploughed field. This woman of the soil would go on to become Maithili, the lovely princess of Mithila. Also called Sita, she would reign as the queen of the prosperous Ayodhya. The merchant had a premonition that Sita would be none other than Goddess Lakshmi in human incarnation. This beautiful mustard sari had been created for that Sita, with great dedication of a devotee and the brilliance of an artist.

In her youth Sita would be married off to Rama, the heroic and valiant prince of Ayodhya. With the turn of events, the majestic princess and her husband would be exiled from their kingdom by the cruel conspiracy of the dominant queen mother, Kaikeyi. While in exile Sita would face tremendous misfortune, resulting in catastrophic wars. The merchant got his gift for the graceful Sita woven with magical powers, which would shield the divine woman from evil intrusion. He insisted the labour of his devotion be passed on to Sita as a part of her wedding trousseau.

His honest confession though attracted nothing but mockery. People considered his obsession to be the mania of a creative mind. The royal women of Mithila were jealous and angry. The most exquisite piece of garment, which took several years to be woven in its majestic design, was meant for someone who was to be born thousands of years later! Could there be something more silly? Disgruntled and disappointed, the intricate sari crafted for Princess Maithili with supreme care and panache was returned.

The heartbroken merchant did not take kindly the royal family's refusal to accept his masterpiece for the future heir. He treated the return as a rejection, an insult to his craft! The merchant was unable to bear the fate of his revered handiwork. Instead of taking it back to his inventories, he chose to place it at the feet of the almighty, to finally relieve himself of the agony, for which he travelled the distance to attend Gautam's fire sacrifice. He stood aloof all through the festivities, engaging but not necessarily immersing in the rituals. He managed to sacrifice the ambitious fabric but not the humiliation it had brought him. His body was captive in the present, while his mind had travelled to the future and his eyes had viewed what the rest of the world couldn't possibly fathom.

The gossip made for a good audience. But when the sari was passed on to me I was so caught up in its gorgeous spread and stunning colours that I failed to read into the curse of an artist and, perhaps, even the sigh of the yet-to-be-born queen. The naughty winds passed again, prophesying that many years later this merchant would be reborn as Lakshmana, the trusted younger brother of the prince of Ayodhya and Sita's husband, Rama. Lakshmana would go on

AHALYA

to become a loyal governing force for the divine couple. He would accompany like a shadow, the great Rama, the King of Kings, when he would come to oblige my life with a vital influence, in the distant future.

I ignored the obnoxious forecast. Neither did it insist that I pay any attention to its gibberish. Laughing in silence it twirled away.

Late in the night when everyone had left and Gautam was fast asleep after a bone-wrecking day, or so I thought, I stealthily got up and draped the sari around, arranging the folds and stretches perfectly. The huge moon shone bright outside, drowning the forest, our hut and the rugged path in front. The mystique was calling to step out of my terrestrial bindings and merge with the heavenly aesthetic. I walked out to bathe in glory. Some holy, hypnotic music was playing through my veins as I walked fearlessly towards the forest. Chunks of clouds flew all across the sky, clutching to and separating from each other swiftly, as if patience would cause stagnancy! I was lost in the race above when stealth footsteps from behind frightened me out of my fantasies. I turned. Gautam was standing behind, unhesitant and relaxed. He looked ethereal. His body radiated masculine charm, his muscles shone in splendour, his eyes glowed with celestial desire. He had woken up to the sultry Nature, allured by the sensuous provocations of this hour. Hands outstretched, he invited me to join in the exhilaration, as if beyond this there was nothing.

I stared in awe. This wasn't the Gautam I had known!

My feet felt fixed to the ground. A gush of cool breeze flirted around, caressing us both. It passed through the sleepy leaves of midnight to generate the murmur of the mystique. The moonlight made its way through the obstructing trees and adorned us with light and shade. His vision seemed to gently touch my eyes and penetrate my soul. For once I wanted to submit to him without any apprehension, waiting for him to take the evening ahead, unlike other nights when I was in command. Gautam knew all about the frame of my body, having diligently been taught its secrets by me. This evening was a test for all his skills, which Gautam seemed more than willing to take with great delight. With steady confidence he walked forward slowly, each step soaked in lustful devotion. He went past me to stand behind, his breath falling heavy on the right of my neck. His chest touched the bare of my back gently. I shivered. His hand came around and rested on the side, digging my skin softly with the tip of his fingers. This time the touch wasn't intimidating; it was empathetic and caring. It felt as if Gautam's fingers were applying layers of sandalwood on my blazing skin, its pleasant fragrance spreading through the forest and moistening my feverish body. I felt like a queen, the fairest and the richest living on Earth.

Strangely this evening Gautam wasn't in haste. He was relaxing and enjoying. He didn't want this evening to pass as much as I! He spent time watching and reeling, appreciating my presence around him. Notoriously he came around to make me conscious of my own body. With him I was exploring passion all over again, getting to know myself in a manner I had never done before. For the first time I felt loved. Love, like a tornado, which can blow apart, yet you fear no one because nothing in the world would protect you more than the arms of a lover. We seemed to fly with our feet strongly grounded. Clouds hovered over the moon as we stood facing each other, not sure when our shields had fallen. Unpretentious and unmasked we presented ourselves to each other, the beauty of being ceremoniously announced amongst the vast expanse of Nature. Our closeness was the loudest declaration of our wedding, far more truthful than the kindling fire on the banks of Mandakini, the fire that wedded us following the commandment of Lord Brahma.

12

With a rare commitment our hands and lips pleasured each other, redefining ourselves like nymphs of the night. The fragrance of sandalwood on my body was increasingly getting dominated by a stronger smell emanating from a foreign source, the origin of which couldn't be Gautam. I was aware of that smell, but each time I tried to place it, it slipped away. Before me, in the visible world, Gautam wore that reckless, raunchy scent, soaked in rugged masculinity. I seemed to recognize this fragrance as if it were embedded deep somewhere in the lost turns of memory. It was trying to remind me of something. Something I had visited in my past.

Something that was woven intensely with the very purpose of my being. Something that was beyond my mortal expanse starting with birth and ending with death. This was far more profound and magnificent. For a split second I think I saw restless branches coiling out of a majestic trunk, surging into the clouds. Little shiny stars came rushing to fill that part of the sky, deterring my probe and rebuking my disobedience. I wanted to clutch on to that image and walk back into history to locate it. But the abstract impressions did nothing more than tease my alertness, bestowing me with metaphysical visuals I could only half-recognize, because a smoky curtain fell in between by some cosmic mischief. Yet, my subconscious returned the hazy view of a divine tree, curved spectacularly at its edges, spiralling upwards with its beautiful little leaves and orange flowers, where tiny blue birds flocked to suck nectar.

Frustrated with this unnecessary, confusing disposition, venturing somewhere between light and dark, I slowly walked backwards only to collide with that strong, raunchy smell which led me towards the unfulfilling vision. I turned with a frown. With a seductive smile Gautam invited me back from the reverie. I lifted my hands to touch him; he moved two steps behind. I walked forward. Like a shadowy ripple he pushed afar and brought himself closer, being delinquently available at all moments from all sides, yet not granting me the pleasure of acquiring.

He would lean on me from the right, pull me towards himself from behind with a strong grip on my waist and suddenly touch my shoulder from the left, his eyes and mouth dangerously close to mine. But just as I would try to reach out, he'd withdraw swiftly and make an advance from another angle, taking me by complete surprise. I allowed him to carry on with the game till I astonished him with a sudden fling of my hands girdling his neck, rendering him motionless. Gautam held me very close to him and laughed at being outwitted so ruthlessly. The echo of his laughter reached up to the clouds, splitting them with thunderous sounds. Lightning cracked through the divide.

This transformation of Nature was not frightening. Nature did not erupt to spurt its fury. This was rather the celebration of lovers where victory lay in accepting defeat. With the side of his face he touched mine, his breath hot like lava burning my cheek. His lips caressed my neck. Seeping in desire, my eyelids closed to block the distracting vision. The mind wanted to see this moment much more than the eyes could desire. As his chin dug into my nape Gautam let his fingers pass softly over my spine. My skin was aroused to the passion at the wake of this magnetic invitation.

At one moment it felt like I had known this man for ages, as if he had touched me before, this yearning I was accustomed to, his playful ploys were firmly embedded somewhere in the core of my subconscious. I opened my eyes to investigate who this person was, haunting the memory with some obscure irrelevant clues. Gautam opened his eyes too, to inspect the source of the distraction. The very next moment he took me by shock as his fingers entered uninvited to fiddle with the delicate, confirming to himself and to me that even my distractions from him were governed by none other than him.

Lost in each other we set ourselves free. The soft grass tickled our skin as we let ourselves fall on its bed. Gautam effortlessly climbed over me, his hands clasping mine at the wrist. With a notorious smile I tried to shove him aside. But this evening his balance was impeccable. Not for once did his focus deviate. He had approached me today as the man of wonders, a clandestine lover who had hidden his passion under covers of thick opaque smoke, whose proximity at this hour was as surreal as the music of a hundred thousand nymphs. The walls in his mind seemed demolished by the unflinching force of the ardent lover, overwhelmed to take possession of himself and me with absolute honesty. A drop of tear trickled down as Gautam formalized our union at the climax. Our wet bodies hugged each other on the ground, seeking tranquil repose. But the night wasn't over yet.

Before this dreamy stretch of the evening

could sink in, he held out his palm inviting me to follow him for another divine expedition. We walked together hand in hand, my head resting on his shoulder, his chin touching my forehead and our steps matching up comfortably with unfamiliar cadence. Through the narrow shadowy path contoured by dark red blooms with fireflies flocking on to them, we reached Mandakini. Her waves swelled and lashed as the moon cast its glitter on the water. Our feet sank into the sand, every step ahead being a deliberate effort to pull out from the gliding earth and make progress. On the bank of the river we stopped. The breeze passed through the heated particles of our bodies, cooling our nerves but calming not a thing. We looked at each other with an urge as if we had met our soulmate transcending many births. As if we were two virgins waiting to be taken for the first time ever, our bodies throbbing with the pain of suppressed passion. As if there were no past that had ever cast its influence on the path, we had jointly created for ourselves. As if there were no future ahead which we desired to blossom. These moments were exclusive, unbounded by time or weather. The present was ours in spirit and being, and we wrote the course of its miraculous flow with great commitment, clutching against each other with faith of inseparability.

Hands wet with ice-cold water touched my midriff. I looked back to acknowledge the presence of the offender and fell on his chest, my face hidden into the crevice from where I could hear the throbbing beats. He lifted a hand to touch my chin and get my eyes transfixed back on his. The other hand went downwards, sending tremors below my feet. The sand welcomed us again.

We descended on the moist ground. Deprived of its peaceful slumber the Earth woke up to our moans. Large chunks of clouds passed in haste, bonding and parting in glee, as the breeze chased them across the vast sky. Fatigued, and yet not fulfilled, we held on to each other like a snake engirdles the night queen. Gautam's mouth lowered on my lips, caressed my neck and stroked my shoulders. At some unguarded instant I pushed him off and hauled myself above to take control. Astonished with my unexpected triumph he let his fingers slide across my waist rendering me powerless. On his tough shoulders I lay my head, our skin touching each other like the souls they held were one, united for life and beyond. Mandakini pulled us towards herself. We let ourselves lose on the bed of pebbles over which the serene water passed. The cold soothed our intense nerves; diffused minerals restored our energies. Currents of the river stretched and pushed with its inherent command, to strengthen back our worn-out muscles.

Strange it was that I did once seek refuge of Mandakini after that terrible night when Gautam had ransacked my fantasies and savaged through my body. The same person held me with care this night, titilating through my being with tantalizing sensations and leaving behind the much-desired exhaustion. Love makes you look at life with a glittery sheen. Love makes you perceive beauty. Else why would the skeletal structure, the detached eyes, the thin ribs, which once felt like the remorse of the befallen, now feel like the bounteous banyan that can shelter my dreams like none other ever can. Gautam's presence in my world once felt like the interference of an imposter; his cold aloofness was enraging as it humiliated my cheerful attendance. The same person had today come back to me like the most generous blessing of the universe, his mirth shining like the King of Gods!

My thoughts were interrupted by long fingers touching the side of my neck. I smiled. For one last time Gautam brought himself over me, his lips pleasuring with lustful, insatiable impatience. I caressed his shoulder muscles with my palm and ran my fingers over his spine. His body was blazing with wild energy, galloping through the unexplored with the unwavering concentration of a royal horse. Closed doors flung open for him as do the rusted temple gates when pervaded by stormy winds. With princely valour he entered again and conquered, overwhelming himself and me by giving rather than acquiring. At the pinnacle of pleasure, we were liberated of every force that had held us away from each other.

We held each other in our arms and slipped into deep sleep by the river. Having shed all inhibitions and indulged in a night of intense fantasies altering life and the living, our bodies retired like there was no tomorrow. Mandakini kept washing our feet.

13

I opened my lethargic eyes when the sharp rays of the sun accused me of irresponsible indolence.

The previous night's passion lingered all over the place, still playing a bohemian music amid bounteous nature. I slowly turned towards my side. Gautam was not there! I scanned around, expecting him to be smiling in affection at my drowsy face. But on the banks of Mandakini where waves splashed like a playful child, at the desolate edge of the forest afar, on the vacant path that lead to the hermitage, memories appeared in colourful stains, but the man himself was nowhere to be seen. Where could he be gone, I wondered, sulking at the way I had been discarded after a romantic extravagance. Was he back to his hermitage to start a regular day? Was he preparing himself for the morning offerings? Had he washed his porch already and installed the iron *kunda*? But why did he leave alone when we had just pledged for unflinching togetherness for all the years to come? Did he try to wake me up from my slumber? After being satiated with overpowering ecstasy did I just ignore his calls to revival with idle inattention?

A pang of guilt passed through my timid heart. I sat up with a start on the sand. Quickly I took my bath and wrapped the silly cloth around. The beautiful mustard and beetroot-violet border looked pale at this hour, perhaps warning me of lost glamour and glory. The sari hadn't remained the same, nor did I. Neither did the time which crafted the most pleasant hours of my life. Gautam's touch from the night before still felt fresh. But the loneliness of the morning, dehydrated by the crude rays of the sun, alerted that something indeed had changed drastically. I ran towards the hermitage in haste. The disciples waited there, confused. The porch wasn't washed. The kunda lay unprepared in a corner. I stood dishevelled, unprepared for the day to take its course. And Gautam had disappeared.

Confused with the eerie absence and strange isolation amidst the crowd, I gathered myself for damage control. The disciples lent a helping hand. My heart pounded with a forecast of impending danger, perils of which promised to be deeply menacing. With every passing hour remnants of the night before were rapidly turning into a distant memory. I could do least to hold it back, still seeking refuge in those moments of love, praying with all my might that life didn't end there. I could still feel Gautam all over my skin. His bones, his muscles, the chest, his hands encircling my waist, his lips teasing every secret softness – the ethos of romance came rushing like ruthless floods. I looked around once again. The nature, barren and dry with only a vulture taking its rounds far above, confirmed my fears. Something dark was indeed looming large.

Everyone left eventually. The fire wasn't kindled on our porch. Unable to bear this unprecedented pause after a fantastical night I set out in search of the sage. After hours of self-defeating traverse, I found him fallen below a peepal, his tall domination crumpled like broken glass scattered into pieces. He opened his eyes upon hearing my footsteps. He had been expecting me. With the cold of a wolf waiting for attack, he sat up in disgust.

'Indra!' he roared. 'Indra it was.'

I stood frozen observing this hopeless contrast in his attitude. The torso on which I leant yesterday to feel the warmth and hear the rhythm of life looked obstinate. Eyes shamed with the recollection of wild lovemaking wanted to dismiss everything about it. Voice rough, hair unkempt, he ruthlessly insulted the time that I considered to be the most delightful endowment of my youthful verve. But my precious, was his sin!

'Brahma did warn me of your power to invoke Indra, but my confidence brushed aside all warnings till it was way too late to prevent the disaster. I am left with nothing today, my carefully crafted pursuits leading nowhere. I will have to start again from scratch, jinxed woman.' He lamented.

Disaster! Did he just call it a disaster? I shuddered thinking whether I let my body be pleasured by an unstable intelligence which fell to temptation once and now held the world responsible for his escapade. How could he not feel tranquilled by the night before? Having been touched by the subtle, how could he return to this self-engrossed aggression? On dust he remained laden, shunning the pebbled riverbed like corrupt opulence.

I grimaced. He hardly noticed.

'You got him to enter me when I wasn't conscious.' Gautam accused me, a finger nastily pointed at me. 'He played his cunning tricks, intruding the solemn path I had created with care. I hadn't realized when he had pulled me far away from my quests, my wisdom massacred, restraints plundered, promises of renunciation vanquished. The purpose I pursued with uncompromising diligence lies scattered and distanced with few weak moments of foolish carelessness.' He wailed.

Unable to comprehend the figure on whom he entrusted the liabilities of his distractions, I stood there confused and looked at the fallen grace with sardonic pity. Gautam still looked lost, hopelessly blabbering to himself.

'Indra had been there all through, attracted to the beauty that Brahma generously bestowed upon you. He followed you to Earth when you travelled from Heaven. He remained camouflaged as your pain, your tears, as the smell of the lavender, in the wetness of the dew. I didn't recognize him!'

This name, repeatedly appearing in Gautam's complaints, echoed through my subconscious like the shrill sound of metal each time it hits the ground. This was someone I should have remembered but could not. I felt restless. A sense of déjà vu played, potent enough to seek attention but too slippery to cling on to. I looked back at Gautam, expecting more information.

'Indra. The force behind *indriya*, the senses.

The corresponding reactions.' He tried to explain in short, incomplete sentences, the deficiency of words left in the care of enraged expressions. 'Indra, the King of Gods. The one who brings rains to Earth. The representative of five indriyas governing the minds of humans. A provocation. An unholy invitation. The source of emotions, attachments, responses.' Gautam was almost talking to himself with a lunatic disorientation, his eyes hysterically searching for some lost treasure which had just been stolen out of his reach. I was still not sure where all this were coming from. The frantic fecklessness was overbearing and too difficult to stand and watch. I walked ahead and touched him from behind, urging him to calm down. He cringed as my fingers came in contact with his skin. He looked at me again. The lethal fire in eyes desired to transform the Earth into my pyre.

'Gaining control over the indriyas had been my penchant of a lifetime. For days and nights, I worked on myself and on the nature beyond to restrict and liberate. In detachment lay my power.

I was rising steadily above mediocrity, gaining that neutral vision of the world, which isn't limited by what the eyes see, the ears hear, or the skin feels. Beyond the confinement of the indriyas lies the real world which isn't driven by mortal conditions. That's the ultimate freedom. That's revolutionary. That's immortality.'

He raised his finger at me once again, swaying fiercely in the air, brutally piercing my skin even from a distance, with allegations of obscenity, of blasphemy. 'Indra is my enemy. Falling into the conspiracy of the indriyas was a catastrophic blow to years of labour. Everything I ever built stands ruined, forsaken and forbidden! All because, Ahalya, you made friends with him!'

'Friends with whom? I have never wanted a single human being other than you …!' Accused enough of sacrilegious motives, I couldn't hold back any further.

My sincere confession irked the sage even more. 'You cannot want me. You cannot desire me,' he roared. 'I am a hermit. I am not supposed to be the illusion of beauty. My presence is spiritual and timeless. But you ... you destroyed it all. That's what illusion does. It criminally dismantles the castle of truth.'

'But how? Am I not your wife?' I still tried to reason, treading my voice out of the initial shock. Gautam nodded his head slowly, his eyes still violently focused on me.

'The wife of a recluse doesn't pursue pleasure. Our journey was supposed to be a divine unison where we dedicate ourselves for the greater good, beyond our humanly instincts. Our bodies were to unite without attachment. Our souls were to bond for a giving that causes welfare to others, not selfishly and materialistically benefit ourselves. When our power was to enhance with joint dedication, all we did was to exalt our weakness by desiring each other's bodies.' He said sadly.

'Rising beyond the self was the journey.' He sighed deep and long and charged again. 'You brought that vice upon me. You summoned Indra to take over me with your hidden powers to invoke the indriyas. You created the path for Indra to enter my body and overshadow my pursuits.

With your guile. With your beauty.' Bitterly he added, perhaps hating himself for the fallen grace much more than all his wrath hurled against me.

I didn't know who this Indra was. But I couldn't protest either. The name, Indra, my powers to arouse him in another being, his competence to take over offering luxurious extravagance, the godly intervention between my love for life and Gautam's ambitious afterlife – a celestial music strung these in a magical garland entwining clumsily around my bun. It touched my neck, fell on my shoulders, tickled my back. There was a strange pull for going back to where I belong, leaving Gautam alone with the tales of his downfall.

Gautam may have noticed that. No shame or guilt must have shown on my face, because there was none. It was relieving rather to know that this wasn't the person I had loved. Well, not exactly. There was a spirit of happiness and lustre, which still remained in hiding. But the whining, self-destructive force before me was set to ruin all that he possessed, in blind pursuit of everything that he didn't. In my own freedom my heart had discarded this dead soul, preparing to start again from scratch to search that source of life which Gautam lamely accused to be within my grip.

'Your devotion was an invitation for him to stalk you till here.' Gautam resumed, his eyes fuming with anger. Startled I looked up. Indra had been stalking me! Why didn't he appear before me then in all his grandeur? Why didn't he take possession of me, sweeping me off my feet, away from a husband so absorbed in his own cause that the wife's felt like a humiliation? Where was this Indra when I was prepared to present myself before the lover like a dew-washed leaf in the morning? Was this the call of love and longing that erupted in fragments within my subconscious, playing notoriously with my urges of dark nights, unwilling to end the chase with disciplined submission?

The voice of the sage interrupted again like a rant through my chain of thoughts.

'Your soul had longed for him even before Brahma had given you a body. Like a parasite he built himself to control your mind and senses. Inspired by his guile you did the same to me, Ahalya! You forced me out of consciousness, planting within my heart the seeds of desire. When my spiritual powers were weak, Indra entered me and made me run towards my ruin. The penance I practised for all these years stand wasted.'

'What you are talking about is pure human instinct. That is what keeps the world and its beings together. Affection isn't disgrace, attraction isn't sin.' My disinterest in Gautam now shone as my confidence, irking the sage more.

What a strange situation I had been thrown into! A husband who treats me like an obstacle to his path of achievements. A divine lover who remains in hiding but influences my choices, my responses and my desires. Torn apart between the reality that I didn't want and the fantasy I couldn't reject, I was trapped within dubious factors of morality which made me furiously loyal to the lover, yet the world would remember me for my deceit. My eyes burnt. The blood in my veins rebelled. From the depth of my heart a yearning released its silent vociferous invitation.

Indra ... Indra ... Indra ...

14

The breeze stopped, shocked. The bold voice of silence prepared to travel its indistinct path through trees and mountains and clouds to carry a message to my only true lover. If anyone other than me would be convinced of my integrity, it must be he. But before my urges made their way to the destination Gautam stood blocking the way. He pronounced his last resort to tame me of my repulsive shamelessness.

'You, Ahalya, will now suffer the same fate as I. You stripped me of my consciousness; you would be left here alone, ripped apart from your senses. Like a stone you will lie on the hard earth, inert and dormant. Lifelessly you would have to wait here watching the world, unable to react. The awareness of your beauty that rides your thoughts and actions with pompous snobbery will abandon you. Like a rock you would remain fallen, separated from the *indriyas* that have been the force of attachment between you and Indra!'

Taken aback by the undeserving curse I stared at Gautam with deep shock. But then what was so shocking? Hasn't power always made its best attempts to uproot voices? I lacked the strength to protest. He sat up slowly as he spoke, his eyes ravaging like a thousand fallen destitute. 'May you forget all about the form you are so boastful of. Surviving thus you would merit yourself no more importance than an ordinary rock, taking upon yourself the damages of time for ages to come, till Lord Vishnu sets his foot on this hermitage to set you free.'

From the ground he raised himself tall again, as if pronouncing the curse had granted him solace and renewed vigour. With monarchical arrogance he walked back unscathed towards his reclusive life, discarding me like the scandal of one night. He left behind a recollection of all those seductive moves which made me sigh for more only a few hours ago, those that had now been declared as unpardonable immoral offence.

A loud hiccup brought me back to myself. The curse had started working. Something inside me struggled to come out. It felt like a lump that refused to leave, but a strong force worked on it from outside.

And in those few moments a haze cleared – the haze of illusion that allows us to look at life in broken bits and parts, the haze that filters some events to the forefront binding them into memories and pushing everything else aside to be dumped into the subconscious. At that moment my conscious met the subconscious. Surprised, I looked back at Gautam. He was walking away in long strides, oblivious of the fact that the clarity he was seeking with all his withdrawal from materialistic pleasures was mine now by virtue of a curse. He didn't know what he was leaving behind eternally. As my human responses prepared to turn inert, an acute awareness of the surreal grew more overwhelming. I saw everything with utmost precision. I saw the past and I saw glimpses from the future. I saw Indra!

The river, the rains and the mist were all agents of Indra, his aides. Right from the time when Brahma had declared his desire to carve the most beautiful woman, Indra had activated his allies to partner with Brahma. Brahma was not to be lured by womanly advances. He remained an obsessed artist, disconnected from the rest of the world. The call of the river and the rains fell flat on him. But Brahma could not keep off their creative influence onto his magic. With rich tools he cast my face and body, unknowingly embedding into them the unpredictability of the rains, the adventure of the river and the mystery of the mist. Unable to convince Brahma of its womanly longings, the river had uttered a curse. *It's more dignified to lash on a rock and fall scattered than engaging with Brahma.* The rains disclosed similar contempt. *In spite of all her attempts to engage Brahma, he remained undeterred like the opaque of a rock.*

AHALYA

Brahma was not the one to be touched by curses. His natural glow burnt everything. The curses hovered around till he created me. And like all progeny that inherits the responsibilities and burdens of their father, the curses fell on me. Ruthlessly they appeared claiming their due as soon as Gautam pronounced his furious ultimatum.

I would be reduced to the existence of a rock, unable to perceive or return perceptions.

Such irony is life! Didn't Brahma once boast that my life wouldn't be confined within the dictum of destiny? That I wasn't born out of the desire between couples but from the imagination of the artist, which would grant me the freedom from inheritance? Contrasting his forecast, I'd now have to bear the curses of the father which were waiting like the debts of a lifetime. Brahma was right in philosophizing, 'The indomitable spirit of creation is, you can create only a part of your vision; the rest creates itself!'

With a soul-baring thrust, something was trying to escape from my insides. It made its way out finally and I choked. My senses just abandoned me, taking with them my desires to touch, feel, live, love. Like black clouds they travelled upwards in the air and disappeared. A dubious transparent sheen in front split into a thousand pieces. Standing on the same ground I could now see much more, across all phases of time.

Consciousness dawned over me like early rays of the sun after an overcast night.

I looked back again. Gautam had gone so far now that even if I called out to him he wouldn't hear. His angry steps encased with pride didn't know that he was leaving behind a prized possession. His curse had not only taken from me my strength to love and seek love but also taken from him his richest treasure and bestowed it on me – the faculty of detachment! I turned back to face the world ahead with a clear and unbarred vision. The horizon opened up for me, the past, present and future appearing in graphic sheens one after the other.

I saw the Kalpavriksha on which I rested once.

Those days when Brahma wasn't done with my making, I had shed tears, I had seen the beauty of colours, I had smelt of something rugged and erotic – it felt reckless and raunchy. The same fragrance came back to me on the banks of Mandakini, when Gautam and I were making love!

Indra!

So divinely close and yet so playfully apart. He had been chasing me even before I had a body. Without Brahma's permission he bestowed me with senses. With possessive exuberance he had been pursuing me without my knowledge, owning me as the partner transcending time. The moment I had approached the Kalpavriksha, Indra girdled like an invisible serpent, wrapping himself around me to inseparability. He charmed me with his gifts of illusion. He facilitated me to admire those orange flowers, pollen, blue birds and their melodious chirrups. So engrossed was I in that bond that I didn't hear the storms of destruction threatening us of our togetherness. Neither did Indra bother to pay heed till the Mist warned me of an impending devastation and took me under her shelter. Indra allowed me to be taken away, but not before he had established a secret rapport with my intelligence. He created a magic path to enter my subconscious whenever he desired, reminding of our mysterious love that blossomed on the branches of Kalpavriksha.

Indra settled within me as empowered indriyas, which enthralled me and eventually destroyed Gautam.

When I was sent to Earth, Indra remained with me in his illusory invisibility. The beauty I tried to create around me was he. Through the flowers with which I decorated Gautam's hut, the trees I planted, my efforts to clean, to build and to nurture, he manifested himself. When I bathed in Mandakini he flirted by throwing ripples mischievously at me. He helped me discover paradise as I sat alone on the banks, seeking pleasure of the body all by myself.

And then there was a morning when my carelessness had made me stand almost bare before Gautam. He saw what no other man in his physical form had ever seen before.

AHALYA

Enraged and jealous Indra had wreaked havoc that evening. He marched through Nature in fury, raised a catastrophe through the landscape, rushed chaotically, driving insane the waves of Mandakini, uprooted the neem tree I had once planted with great fondness and blew away the roof sheltering us, punishing me with ice-cold downpours that pierced my body like needles. The Mist came to protect me; he pushed her aside and roared hostile from behind the thunder.

It was the following morning when Brahma informed that I must marry Gautam. He believed the alliance would be the best conspiracy to separate me from Indra. Hadn't the King of Gods tricked Father always, owning me much before Father had even breathed life into my sculpture? I was quickly married off to the sage when the enraged lover was away. By the time the sacrificial fire of our wedding reached Heaven to seek divine blessings, it was too late. Furious once again at my callous consent, Indra stood apart in wrath watching me suffer the rampage with Gautam on our first night. But my tears and the suffering must have pained him too. With sadness in his heart he smiled mercy and prompted me to invoke himself within Gautam with the power of my indriyas.

At an opportune moment he slithered into the body of the sage, making him do things he hadn't ever attempted before. Inch by inch Indra gathered control over Gautam's consciousness, slowly replacing his restraints with indulgence. The hermit who never looked back when I travelled a gruelling journey from Heaven to Earth had started treating me with kindness. As I got closer to Gautam with each passing day Indra too gathered his ground with proprietary influence, hiding behind the mask of penance.

And finally, the night arrived when Indra was at the peak of desire. Repeatedly he emptied himself inside me, pleasuring and numbing my energies simultaneously. As I looked back in time, I saw him clearly now! Hair strewn behind like feathery clouds, strong hands that wrapped my neck like an encompassing shield, body bare. Gallant, muscular and radiant, he stood behind the pale

Gautam, his eyes smiling with notorious glee. His chest broad and physique tall had threatened to burst the sage to pieces. On that enchanting evening he had come out of the boundaries of Gautam's body to stand by himself. When I dug my face into his chest, I hadn't noticed the different person I was making love with. He may have laughed at my innocence and ignorance as I remained drowned in the sea of desire. The reality of Gautam was cast aside; I played along with the illusion of the indriyas. That illusion was Indra!

Ravishing sensuousness had provoked hypnotic arousal that was not to fade away anytime soon. With masculine force he had bestowed upon me the most incredible pleasure a woman can seek.

And as the Mist had warned once, I too had fallen into a timeless sleep after the copulation. Indra had discarded Gautam like a tattered cloth and returned to where he belonged.

His mighty revenge on Gautam was to let the sage discover that I had been triumphed by the one I deserved to be with. With bitter sarcasm he was left alone to unravel his failures. Neither could he satisfy his wife nor could he prevent her from being pleasured the way she desired. Could there be a bigger insult to a man than an obstinate, ambitious wife unwilling to yield to unfair sacrifices? Since the limitation of a man is always explained as the failure of his woman, I too stood there bearing the consequences, discarded and disowned like a barren rock, observing much more than what I did till a while back but feeling nothing! No anger, no hatred, no disgrace, no hurt.

Gautam had pronounced a curse against Indra too; I am not sure what. My body has now started to feel stiff, paralyzed of the sensation that the passing breeze or the restless stream must cause. They touch me gently and then by force in an attempt to set me in motion, as they do to any other stationary object. But my legs feel increasingly heavy, strongly grounded, perhaps a part embedded in the dense soil. Through heat and rain and chill I am meant to stand, attending to the passage of time but affected by none, as one season follows the other and the blooms change colours. My supple milky skin must curdle in the days to come, taking with it the beauty of sandalwood and rose that Brahma had so carefully crafted me with.

Held inert by the body, my mind turns far more active. And observant. I see Nature and its ploys. I see life as a whole, a balance between happiness and sadness, achievements and failures, originalities and artificialities. I see Heaven and Underworld, with Earth adjusting dangerously between the daunting dark and the glowing brightness. The past is clear now. With all the elements threading in perfectly to explain my present, there is more for me to explore. Though I can't particularly feel or express any further with distinct clarity, the new-found consciousness empowers me to see the future.

A future that is no less eventful than my momentous and turbid past.

15

What Brahma creates, Vishnu sustains.

I can see ages hence Vishnu would appear on these premises in his human incarnation of Rama. Vishnu, the Supreme Being; the one who knows it all. The deity who resides in the heart of hearts and nothing can ever be hidden from him. The most knowledgeable one, ready to traverse till any extent to unfold the hidden truth.

By then Gautam's hermitage would have turned into a heap of ruins. Not only would the fragile, unkempt hut look haunted but also the wild ingrowth would provide home to bats and snakes and scorpions. The designs on the wall would fade away, my plants would be dead, replaced by unruly creepers mightily celebrating the mound they'd make out of my hut. All those little things I once did to build a home with soil and hay would be lost somewhere in time, its presence to be felt only in folklore.

Mortals would be advised not to walk through those ruins, lest Ahalya's curse befalls them too. Grandparents would tell stories to their grandchildren, of a beautiful and greedy woman named Ahalya – perhaps a *Yakshi*[7] in disguise – who had taken a pious sage on the path of sin. Well, almost. 'Ahalya's unfulfilled desires, her ghostly sigh of pain, still pass through the breeze of those ruins.' They'd tell the little ones to steer clear from the abandoned hermitage.

Gautam left me, but he would never ever settle again. He would keep travelling across the length and breadth of the country, through forests and remote localities, from Mithila to the banks of Narmada and Godavari, to Pushkar and Kailash, stopping nowhere for long. He would subject

---

[7] Yakshi: female Yaksha, a nature spirit. Mention found in Hindu, Buddhist and Jain mythology.

himself to rigorous penance to please the Gods and gain back the status of Maharishi. He would take holy dips in the rivers, immerse himself to work towards the welfare of the world, and help people overcome their miseries and ailments. He would educate the uncultured, train the aborigines, dig ponds where water is scarce, pick up the plough and tame the cow to raise grains in dry farmlands. He would draw many disciples on his travels. But he would never encourage them to follow him in his journey. Gautam would prefer to be left alone, lest some form of Maya lure him again into the illusion of attachments. Me, he would never forget, and himself he'd never be able to forgive.

After years of self-defeating hard work to service mankind, Maharishi Gautam would find space in permanence among the seven sages in the construct of the constellation called Saptarishi.[8]

---

[8] **Saptarishi:** In Indian mythology, the seven central stars of Ursa Major that form the cup shape are referred to as Saptarshi, meaning seven (sapta) sages (rishis). These are Vasistha, Bharadvaja, Jamadagni, Gautama, Atri, Visvamitra

He would be blessed with immortality. Wasn't this a desire he spoke about often when we sat together on the porch late at nights, looking up at the star-studded sky? From the huge space above he would look down on Earth, of which I would be no more than a miniscule particle.

In the holy scriptures Vishnu is addressed as the God who separates Heaven and Earth, a characteristic he shares with Indra. Both Indra and Vishnu's incarnation, Krishna, are known to be great lovers. One shrewd, the other divine. Indra's quest as a lover being materialistic, Krishna's, philosophical. Both are God of Illusions. Indra dwells on the beauty of the body – temporary and perishable. Krishna is the beauty of the soul – infinite and permanent. Indra is impulse; Krishna is sublime. Just like water can be both life-saving and destructive, so is its lord, Indra. He takes as much as he gives. Vishnu is the selfless giver; his glory shines as much as he offers.

---

and Agastya. These seven rishis are often mentioned in the later works as typical representatives of the character and spirit of the pre-historic or mythical period.

AHALYA

Those days when Brahma was creating me, perhaps unknowingly he had given my hand to Indra while creating the unparalleled beauty of my body. He overlooked that wherever there is splendour, there is Indra. Father opened the gates to the King of the Gods and tried in vain to close them; it was already too late! How strange is life that even my creator wouldn't have complete control over his creation. Once initiated it rolled by itself.

And now I must wait for Lord Rama to arrive and rescue me. Rama, the avatar of none other than Vishnu. Are Vishnu and Indra friends? Or maybe the foresight and hindsight of time? Are they the conscious and subconscious of the same faith? I don't know.

Years would pass as I would stand strong facing the enormities of Nature. The second queen of Ayodhya, Kaikeyi, would plan a ploy to send the eldest prince to exile for fourteen long years. In those fourteen years Prince Rama would travel through forests and change the world, meeting many such earthlings whose hardships could be put to end only by divine intervention. In due course it would be time for him to cross the same forest where I stand today like a stone. He would be accompanied by his brother, Lakshmana, and wife, Sita.

Lakshmana, the same merchant of garments in an earlier birth, who had woven the mustard sari with a beetroot-violet border. The cloth that was meant to protect Sita from misfortune. It brought misfortune to me rather, for adorning myself with the failed aspiration of an insulted artist. I would recognize them instantly, remembering the forecast of the breeze on that fateful day. Lakshmana would remain distanced, deprived of any memory that could bereave him of the peace of serving his goddess in this birth.

As Rama would walk past, his feet would fall on me. He would stop right there to take a closer look; to look through me. Instantly he would see the truth of my being, covering the entire span of my celestial and terrestrial existence. The Lord's crystal vision would rupture the invisible walls of Gautam's curse to discover the woman again, with all her fragmented components assembled back to form. The innocence of my longing, the stubborn desire, the commitment in my call of love. The overpowering *indriyas*. The romance of Indra. The resistance, indulgence and withdrawal of Gautam. In one blink Rama would witness it all.

His recognition of my truth would set me free.

With Rama's reconciliation the world's perceptions would change almost immediately. Rama's resolve to stand before me in person, allowing me to take a complete look at his earthly form, would invite the world to break its mental blocks. He would heal me of the bruises left by Gautam's insulting allegations, cleansing those dirty scars of infidelity off my skin. No longer would I be remembered as the evil woman who diverted the concentration of a righteous sage. The folklore would start singing hymns in praise of Ahalya Mata, whose purity has earned the blessings of none other than the God who resides inside hearts. The one who remains under the cover of infinite layers of immorality. Only as you shed one by one those amorphous layers inflicted by corrupt intents does the sight of the God get clearer before you. I would see him clearly, all his avatars rolled into one.

Rama. Vishnu. Krishna. Narayana.

His touch would liberate me of all rigidities and earthly judgements, immortalizing me with his lordly blessings. My loyalty towards Indra would secure its due respect.

Forgetting or forgiving Gautam wouldn't matter any longer. Indifference acquired over time would eventually heal whatever I have lost. I would touch and feel again. I would perceive and reciprocate. With all burdens shed on the ever-accepting Mother Earth I would start my reverse journey back to Heaven.

EPILOGUE

As I prepare for the timeless wait of my final return, a visual floats before my eyes from a period to come many years later.

The queen of the infertile king of Hastinapur, Kunti, must bear children to save the kingdom from passing away to evil hands. She is a mathematical genius, possessing the spiritual power to call upon Gods in alignment with the gravitational pull of ruling planets. This would be the time for her to put her knowledge to use, to restore the kingdom and save the subjects. She would have three children from her union with Gods. With bated breath I watch in silence the strange birthing process, from a distance of a few thousand years.

She invokes Indra, the King of the Gods, to bear the child that must possess the intelligence, warfare and creativity of a king. I witness her making love with Indra and giving birth to the warrior prince, Arjun, who would, in due course of time, become a figure celebrated for bringing victory through the greatest war fought on this land. The earth beneath me seems to cave in. I might just fall in and break into a hundred pieces. I sigh. My heart hurts; anger seethes through the folds of my forehead; pangs of jealousy run through my veins.

Arjun could have been my child!

Almost immediately I stand astonished. This wish to bear Indra's child. The hurt. The anger. The jealousy. Where do these come from? Wasn't I supposed to be left inert, devoid of feelings? Consciousness devours me once again, this time accompanied by a drop of tear.

Indra! *Indriya*. The illusion and the senses. The beauty and the longing that comes with it. From some corner of the ethereal world he will keep influencing my life, hiding himself behind the obscure. His hold over my heart is far more compelling than any curse can counter.

Indra will not surrender in love; neither will he let go.

Long, long ago when I was still a novice, seeking an identity without a body, I had asked, 'Would the greatest lover known for his rugged energies make love with the soul?' Indra had forgone his appearance to transform into a shapeless identity, throwing the same challenge back at me and yet fulfilling it in style, beyond the boundaries of time, like no cosmic lover has ever achieved!

Who is Indra? Voices ask me now.

I wish there were words in literature or science to explain his mystery. Indra can only be experienced, never possessed. For some he is a fighter. For others he is a saviour. Some relate with his majestic practices. Many recall him as a seductive lover. And yet others define him as a philanderer. Which of these must be identified as the dominating trait of the Deva, strangely depends on the personality of the interpreter, not Indra's. And it is a woman's relationship with Indra, not with any other man, that determines the strength of her character. Indra is what she feels, Indra is what she makes others perceive, Indra is her senses, Indra is her impulse.

Keepers of historical logs would name me as the first of the *Pancha Kanya*, five virgins. Not that there would be any misjudged reference to prove my celibacy, but neither would there be any insult with allegations of infidelity. Because I have given myself with all my knowledge and truth, my body and mind, to the only one my soul ever connected with. Because my devotion didn't falter over time or under threats. I would be remembered as the philosophical strength of the mortals that would never deflect from her dharma, whatever be the repercussion of her actions on the rest of the world. The moral throne would behold me with pride, along with four other women, who would brave unpredictable demands upon life without compromising on their dignity. Hymns would claim that reciting the names of the Pancha Kanya – the five learned women from Indian mythology

– would dispel sins. Alternative traditions would imprint us on a yet higher pedestal, honouring our devotion and integrity to be among the purest ones that have ever inhabited this planet.

We would be called Sati.

A NOTE TO THE READERS

The *Pancha Kanya*s of Hindu Mythology were Ahalya, Kunti, Draupadi, Mandodari and Tara - while the Five Satis were Sita, Sati, Savitri, Damayanti and Arundhati. The distinction of two different titles arose primarily because various versions of the epics have taken the liberty to celebrate women as per the popular belief of an era and of course, that of the translators. A school of thought defines 'Sati' as the women's unconditional devotion and dependence on their men. They showed the women as loyal followers strongly supporting the vision of their men or helping them to overcome social and emotional complications. These women are depicted as sacrificing and selfless, yet invincible in drafting their own position of strength and supremacy.

Thus, as per textual evidence, the Kanyas and Satis are different women. However, in the old and most original versions, there is no mention of Pancha Satis; they only talk about the Pancha Kanyas who are deemed as the Maha Satis. Even in regional interpretations, especially in some eastern and southern states of the country, this division is blurred. This could be the difference in the spread of Mahabharata of Vedavyasa versus the dissemination of Valmiki Ramayana. The former specifically mentions Pancha Kanyas. Valmiki Ramayana talks about the Satis in terms of loyalty and physical chastity, and such women including Sita aren't restricted to only five. But it doesn't club any of them together under an umbrella term, Pancha Sati. In my own study, I came across some scholarly assumptions that the Satis were reborn as Kanyas and research has tried to draw parallels!

A NOTE TO THE READERS

Popular literature establishes that reciting the name of the Pancha Kanya can dispel sins, which again confirms the 'Sati' status of these women. Sati, meaning pure, devoted, fair. In the Sati series, I shall follow this vision while retelling the stories of the five illustrious women - Ahalya, Kunti, Draupadi, Mandodari and Tara. In Ahalya, I have mentioned the concept of Pancha Kanya and admitted towards the end that Sati is perhaps a different religious construct, but philosophically they merge because both are representations of truth - personal truth of the women for which they are answerable only to themselves, irrespective of external judgements or popular interpretations.

ACKNOWLEDGEMENTS

A book is born not just from a writer's imagination over a few dedicated months. A story is usually born in her heart long before she starts writing it. I must thank those endless story hours from childhood when my mother and grandparents and books engaged me with enchanting stories of glorious kings, powerful queens, lavish jewels, intimidating villains and magical Nature. Those story hours have become my habit, my passion and my profession today.

Indian mythology is philosophically rich and leaves unconditional scopes for interpretation. At a literature festival, while talking about the influence of mythology in my stories, an audience reaction drew my attention to the fact that Lord Indra is

ACKNOWLEDGEMENTS

such a little-explored concept in the literary world. That's where the idea of this Pancha Sati series of books emerged, the first of which is *Ahalya*.

I would always be indebted to such discussions on literature that trigger a writer's imagination and her abilities to challenge the existing binaries.

In the course of my journey with Ahalya, I am immensely thankful to editorial director Prasun Chatterjee and the team at Pan Macmillan India for their confidence and support. Working with Prasun has been absolutely delightful and I am happy that we will be working together on four more books in this series. Many thanks to Rajdeep Mukherjee for bringing us together. I am grateful to Professor Nirmalya Kumar for permitting us to use a painting of Hemen Majumdar on the cover. A big thanks to Misha Oberoi, for coming up with the wonderful cover for the book.

My sincere gratitude, in alphabetical order, for their counsel and recommendations, to Anand Neelakantan, Bibek Debroy, Chitra Banerjee Divakaruni and Namita Gokhale. I sincerely value the questions raised by Namita and insights

ACKNOWLEDGEMENTS

shared by Anand and Mr Debroy, when I needed consultation on certain contexts.

Thanks to my mother, Ratna Dasgupta, who also happens to be the first reader of *Ahalya*, for the long discussion we had and for reorganizing my imagination with her inputs.

My husband Tuhin A. Sinha never reads my manuscripts till they come back in a book form (and vice versa). But during the writing stage, we share ideas and hold house-debates, questioning each other's thoughts, ideas, ideologies. Those are insightful, enjoyable and intense. I thank Tuhin for those moments of discussions on Ahalya and Indra.

Lastly, my gratitude to Neev Tanish, my son – the inspiration that changed me and my life for good! Thanks for putting up with the mood swings of an author-mom.

Before winding up my list of acknowledgements, I sincerely thank all my readers, reviewers and critics, who never failed to reinforce that my stories will be loved and analyzed by a greater audience. I am, because they are.